Knight of My Dreams

Also by Lynsay Sands

An English Bride in Scotland
The Husband Hunt
The Heiress
The Countess
The Hellion and the Highlander
Taming the Highland Bride
Devil of the Highlands
The Brat
Love Is Blind
The Perfect Wife
The Chase
What She Wants
The Reluctant Reformer
Bliss
Lady Pirate
Always
Sweet Revenge
The Switch
The Key
The Deed

Knight of My Dreams

Originally Published under the Title "Mother May I?"

LYNSAY SANDS

AVON
An Imprint of HarperCollins*Publishers*

KNIGHT OF MY DREAMS originally appeared in the print anthology *A Mother's Way*, under the title "Mother May I?"

EPub Edition May 2014 ISBN: 9780062317247

Print Edition ISBN: 9780062317254

10 9 8 7 6 5 4 3 2 1

For Mom

Chapter One

LONDON, ENGLAND
1358

"MOTHER!"

"Oh, dear." Lady Margaret of Fairley paused, then fixed an unconcerned smile on her face and continued brushing her hair as she listened to her son stomp his way through the small sitting room off her bedchamber. By an effort of will, she managed to keep from starting when the door crashed open behind her.

She studiously ignored him as he stormed across the room to where she sat by the fire, but grimaced as she felt him loom above her, breathing fury down the back of her neck.

She waited for a count of ten as he glared and snorted at her much like an angry bull, then glanced over her shoulder and offered a bland smile. "Good morning, son. How are you this fine day?"

The question evidently agitated him. His face flushed an angry red and his expression grew even more furious. Yes, she thought, she could see why the French were terrified of this hulking man. "How am I? How *am* I? God's teeth, woman, how do you think I am?"

"Hmmm," she responded mildly, turning back to the fire. "*Some*one awoke on the wrong side of his bed this morn."

"Not *I!*" he snapped. "I was in a perfectly good mood . . . until my audience with Edward."

Lady Fairley opened her eyes wide, feigning surprise. "Did it not go well?"

"Did it—" He broke off to mutter a few choice words.

She gave him a look of mild reproof. "Please, Jonathan. 'Tis not very chivalrous to speak so around ladies. Are you not a knight of the Order of the Garter? Were you not taught better back when you were a squire? Perhaps instead of sending you to train at Westcott, your father should have taken you in hand—as I suggested. He never would listen to me, that stubborn—"

"Mother," Jonathan interrupted with an obvious attempt at restraint.

"Yes, dear?"

"What did you say to the king?"

"Me?" She stared at him in a show of innocence that merely made his eyes narrow.

"Aye. You. I know you had something to do with this." Judging that it was time to show some irritation of her own, Lady Fairley set down her brush with a clatter. "Something to do with *what*, Jonathan? You have not yet said what has occurred. Why did the king call you here to court?"

She watched the struggle waged on her son's face with interest before he blurted, "He has ordered me to marry! *Me! The Scourge of Crécy!*"

"Oh." She turned back to the fire and resumed tending to her hair. "Is that all? For a moment you had me concerned." She sensed rather than saw the way her son slumped behind her, deflated by her unconcerned response.

"Is that *all*?" he echoed with dismay. "King Edward has given me two weeks to choose my own bride . . . or he will. Two weeks! He wants me married by month's end, *and* to have begotten an heir by next summer." She turned and saw fury suffuse his face at the very thought.

"Oh, bother!" she remarked, drawing his attention back to her.

"Oh, bother?" he repeated.

"Well, really, Jonathan. Do you truly think *I* needed to do anything to bring this about? Ha!" She turned her nose up and sniffed delicately. "It hardly needed my attention, surely? Your father and brother have been gone for five years now, leaving you the lord of Fairley—an *heirless* earl. I am only surprised that King Edward has let the matter go so long. Fairley Castle is on the border of Scotland. Strategically, it is an important keep. Of course he wants you married and your bride bearing. And with all the fighting you do . . . Should you die, the only person to take your place is your cousin Albert. You *know* what a fool he is. So does the king. He would hardly want Albert as lord of Fairley and its lands."

"Well, a babe is scarce likely to do a better job," Jonathan grumbled, shifting irritably.

"No, but if there is an heir and a widow, Edward may put whomever he wishes in your place, either as chatelain, or as a new husband for your bride. Without a widow and heir, Albert will inherit."

Jonathan looked pensive, obviously overcome by the truth of her words, but he scowled as she nonchalantly gave up her brushing in favor of donning jewels and a headpiece. It was her finest headpiece, and one she generally saved for special occasions. Eyes widening slightly, he took in the dress she wore, the way she had pulled up her hair, and . . . Yes, he'd just realized that it was not natural color on her cheeks, but a smuggled French rouge she'd put there. She knew she looked lovely, and younger than her fifty years.

"You are primping!" His words were a dismayed accusation.

Lady Fairley felt herself flush and thought it a rather nice touch as she tried for a slightly guilty expression. "I am not primping," she disagreed with great dignity.

"You are wearing your best jewels."

Beginning to feel her mouth twitch with self-satisfaction, Lady Fairley rose in a display of impatience. "They match my gown. One likes to look one's best at court." She ignored the way he squinted suspiciously at her, and instead of commenting she walked out into the sitting room. Her maid Leda burst in from the hall.

"Here you are, my lady."

"Ah, good," she murmured as the girl rushed forward with a small decanter. Her son watched her take the container, then sniffed suspiciously when she unstoppered it.

"Perfume!" The accusation was shot like an arrow from a bow.

"Aye," she answered, applying it liberally while Jonathan watched in horror. She knew the source of his dismay: she had not bothered to apply perfume since his father had been stricken by the plague. Which was why she had been forced to send her maid out in search of some. She hadn't even brought any with her to court, because there wasn't any from Fairley to bring. All the scent she had once owned had dried up over time. Now it was part of her scheme.

"Thank you, Leda." She handed the perfume back to her maid and continued on to the door, not at all surprised when her son followed.

"Where are you going?" he asked.

"To visit with a friend," she responded gaily.

"What friend?"

"I believe I am past the age of needing to explain myself, Jonathan," she said with mock exasperation. She opened her chamber door, then stepped into the hall. "However, if you must know, I am going to visit with Lady Houghton and her daughter." Seeing the consternation on his face, she fought a smile. This was all going according to plan.

Jonathan had followed her into the hall before comprehension at last dawned on him. She'd convinced the king to order him to marry, and now she would thrust another friend's daughter under his nose! She'd been trying this for years, and he'd managed to sidestep every move to see him wed. In fact, if he never saw another—

"There is no need for you to accompany me," his mother spoke up, ruining his theory quite thoroughly. "In any case, is there not something of more importance that you should be doing? Two weeks is very little time to find a bride—and here at court, things must be doubly difficult. There are many other knights as handsome and accomplished as yourself, my son. If you want to make a good alliance, you really should not waste time following me."

Jonathan was so startled by his mother's pronouncement that he stopped walking and simply gaped at her back. She continued down the hall.

"But what of this friend's daughter?" he blurted at last, hurrying to catch up once he recovered from his shock.

"What of her?"

"Do you not wish me to consider *her* for my bride?"

"Oh, no. She would not do at all."

"What?" He gasped, scandalized. "You have shoved every eligible daughter of every friend under my nose for the last five years. Now here is one you—"

"I have introduced you to every eligible and *suitable* daughter of friends of mine," his mother corrected sharply. "And I have run through the entire list. Now you are on your own."

"You are giving up on me?" he cried, unsure whether to be relieved or injured by such a possibility. Not that he wanted his mother thrusting would-be brides under his nose, but he wasn't sure he wanted her indifference on the subject, either.

"Not at all, son. I shall support you in your choice; I simply can no longer aid you in your quest. Now"—she patted him affectionately on the arm—"go find yourself a bride to please the king, and leave me to my friends."

Jonathan stared at his mother in bewilderment, then he noted that the hand she had patted his arm with was now patting her hair. She was primping again! She hadn't primped since his father's death. Something odd was going on.

"I think I shall accompany you to meet your friend's daughter," he announced as she started away again.

"No!" Lady Fairley shrieked, coming to an abrupt halt. He'd never seen her so agitated. She regained her composure quickly, though, replacing the alarm on her face with an irritated scowl. "I mean . . . I told you she is not suitable."

"Oh?" He eyed her curiously. It had been his experience that nothing short of a questionable virtue was enough to make a woman unsuitable in his mother's eyes. At least lately. To be fair, she had been much choosier at first, when producing possible brides for him to consider, but as the last few years had passed and he had shown a distinct lack of interest in the marital state—especially in comparison to his fighting on the Continent—his mother's desperation had begun to manifest itself. She had begun to parade any woman with all the necessary parts before him. And the "necessary parts" did not always include attractiveness, personality or even all the usual limbs. His mother had grown quite desperate. Virginity had never been a point she overlooked, though. Lady Fairley wanted grandchildren from her own son, not someone else's.

"Is this girl free with her affections?" he asked. His mother turned a horrified expression on him. "Of course she is not free with her affections. Elizabeth raised her properly! The girl is as pure as a babe."

"Hmmm." This was interesting. He found himself intrigued by his mother's vehemence. "Is she betrothed, then?"

Irritation flickered on her face, but she did admit with obvious reluctance, "Nay. Her betrothed was taken by the plague."

"Is she without title or dower?"

Much to his surprise, irritation flickered on Lady Fairley's face once more. "Nay. Her father was a wealthy baron. There is a sizable dower."

"Well, then, why is she unsuitable?"

"She is . . ." Her expression fluctuated briefly, torn between irritation and reluctance as she struggled for an explanation. Jonathan was shocked beyond belief when it finally popped out: "Puffy."

"Puffy?" he echoed with a laugh.

"Aye. She is large. Too voluptuous, if you must know. And she is far too intelligent and strong-minded. She would not do at all. She even reads," his mother added with distaste, giving a delicate shudder. "Nay. She is perfectly nice, but not for you. She—Oh, look! There is Lady

Griselda of Epton. I understand that her parents have not yet secured her a betrothed. Little coin for a dower, I gather," she added in an aside. "But you hardly need concern yourself with that. Why do you not go see how she would suit?"

Jonathan's eyes nearly fell out of his head. He knew quite well that his mother positively loathed the young lady. For some reason, that had once added to the girl's attractions in Jonathan's eyes; he had courted her briefly. Very briefly. The girl had an amazingly high, screeching voice. Which was a shame, really. Otherwise she was quite lovely. Still, a man would have to be completely deaf to put up with her, and Jonathan was far from that.

Of course, Lady Griselda's voice was not the reason his mother did not like her. She claimed the girl was spiteful and sneaky, a heartless witch who wielded gossip as men wielded swords.

Realizing that while he stood there goggling, his mother was doing her best to escape, Jonathan rushed forward. She was moving at a fast clip as she turned the corner ahead. When he followed a moment later, it took him several seconds to spot her. This palace corridor was busier than the one leading to her rooms, and Jonathan suspected that she had put on a burst of speed the moment she was out of his sight. She was a good distance up the hall, half-hidden by a quartet of servants coming toward him.

Proceeding to hurry, himself, Jonathan ate up the distance between them with his longer stride, quickly reaching her side. The glance she threw him was not welcoming. She ignored him as they reached the stairs, then traversed another hall. Finally, at the door he knew led out into the royal gardens, she paused to give him a harassed stare. "Are you not going to go look for a bride? You could hardly wish Edward to choose one for you."

"I have plenty of time for that," he argued. "I want—"

"Oh, aye. Plenty of time," she interrupted scathingly. "A fortnight."

Ignoring her sarcasm, he moved forward and opened the door, gesturing for her to proceed. His mother glared at him in frustration for a moment; then, seeming to realize that he was unaffected by her mood, she let her breath out in a disgruntled whoosh and marched outside.

ALICE WAS THE first to spot the approach of Lady Fairley and her son. At least, Alice assumed it was the woman's son. Margaret of Fairley had spoken a great deal about the man, describing him as tall, dark, and handsome, very strong, solid like his father. She had also given various other flattering descriptions. Most of them appeared correct. He was tall and dark. He certainly looked solid and strong as he marched along beside his much smaller mother. Seeing him, Alice believed everything she'd heard about his campaigns against the French. As for him being handsome, it was hard to say. His face was scrunched up in a scowl as they neared, a scowl that seemed to deepen with every step as his mother verbally berated him.

Alice tilted her head and watched the pair curiously. The petite older woman appeared to be shooing her son away like some pesky fly, her hand waving vaguely in the air as she spoke in aggravated tones to him. The man that Alice assumed to be Lord Jonathan appeared unmoved by her gestures or her words; he followed Lady Fairley forward, pausing whenever she did stop to wave a finger at him, then following again. It was all rather curious, amusing even, and Alice's lips stretched into a smile as she watched the unlikely pair approach.

"What has you so amused?" her mother asked curiously, then followed Alice's gaze. She positively beamed as she espied her friend and the man approaching. "Oh! There is Margaret. And look, young Jonathan has accompanied her."

Alice caught the meaningful expression that her mother cast Uncle James, and had a moment to wonder at it, but then was urged off the bench she occupied.

"Let Lady Fairley have your seat, dear. Respect your elders."

Alice rose automatically and shifted away from the place where her mother and Uncle James were settled. The move made her the first to greet Lady Fairley and her son as they approached.

"Oh, good morning, my dear," the noble woman murmured, and Alice felt her expression reflect her confusion at the cool tone the woman used. Lady Margaret was usually as warm and pleasant as could be. Her coldness now was somewhat startling to Alice and took her aback.

The woman gave the man accompanying her an irritated glance, then introduced him. "This is my son, Jonathan." Her smile was decidedly forced and unenthusiastic. "Jonathan, this is Lady Alice of Houghton."

"Good morn, my lady," he said. The smile that accompanied his greeting was brilliant, making the man's hard face almost handsome as he took her hand and bowed over it.

"Good day, my lord," Alice murmured, smiling politely back even as Lady Fairley added, "He very kindly walked me here, but he cannot stay. He has a task to fulfill for the king."

"Oh, what a shame," Alice murmured politely, her gaze moving curiously from the woman's grim face to that of her again-scowling son. The two staged a silent war with their eyes.

"There is no need for me to rush off right this very minute," Lord Jonathan countered at last. "Certainly, I can afford to spare a few moments to get acquainted with my mother's dear friend and her lovely daughter."

Alice could not help but notice that his charming words merely seemed to agitate Lady Fairley even more. With an exasperated wave, the older woman turned away and almost flounced over to take the seat Alice had just vacated. Apparently the introductions were over. It was hard not to notice and wonder at the fact that Lady Fairley had very obviously neglected to introduce her son to Alice's own mother. Or to her uncle, whom Alice's mother had most mysteriously insisted accompany them on this morning constitutional. Usually her mother was embarrassed by the man, who was something of a court dandy. And more surprising than her uncle's presence, was the sudden warmth that Lady Fairley was showing him. Not that Alice would expect the noblewoman to be rude, but from where she stood, Lady Fairley appeared to be almost gushing over the man, which was entirely bewildering. Alice had not thought the usually dignified woman capable of such effusive feeling, especially over a man like Lord James of Houghton.

Putting this curious turn of events away for later consideration, Alice glanced at Lord Jonathan to find the man glowering at the others with obvious displeasure. Alice peered from son to mother just as Lady Fairley paused in her conversation to glare back at her son and—if she wasn't mistaken—at Alice as well.

"Come stand by me, son. Or better yet, tend to your quest."

Alice gasped at such bossiness, but Jonathan, rather than appearing upset or insulted, just smiled. The smile held a degree of affection, but there was also a median of contrariness. "Nonsense, Mother. I know you are concerned with the completion of my appointed task, but tomorrow is soon enough to start that endeavor. Besides, I can hardly leave Lady Houghton's daughter standing alone here. There is no room for her on that bench you are sharing, so I must stay to keep her company—'tis the chivalrous thing to do. Speaking of Lady Alice," he added slowly, a strange smile coming to his face, "you were hardly fair in your description of her. She is much lovelier than you claimed."

If Alice blushed at this unexpected compliment, Lady Fairley flushed an even redder shade, one that turned almost purple as her son went on: "How was it that you described her?"

Alice peered from son to mother again when Jonathan paused; she was aware of undercurrents here, but didn't understand them.

"You never mentioned that her hair held all the colors of a sunset: mellow golds and fiery reds. Or that her eyes were the clear blue of a cloudless sky. What *was* it you said?" The knight tapped his chin thoughtfully, and all the while his mother grew more straight-backed and tense. Alice simply grew more and more flustered.

"Oh, aye, I remember now. You commented on her figure. What was it you said? She was . . . lush? Round and rich like a berry brought to full ripeness?" Alice wasn't sure how to take such a compliment, but before she could react, Lord Jonathan went on. "No, no. It was something else you said. What was it?"

Lady Fairley looked ready to burst out of her skin. Instead she blurted out, "Oh, go sit over there with her if you insist. Just do be quiet."

He smiled and bowed to his mother, then Lord Jonathan moved to take Alice's arm. He turned her solicitously toward the bench on the opposite side of the path. "Shall we sit over here, my lady? I promise not to embarrass you with any further compliments."

"Er . . . aye. Thank you," she murmured, as bewildered by the exchange that had just taken place as she was flustered by the words this handsome lord had used to describe her. No one had ever described her hair or eyes so prettily, and his description of her figure . . . well, gentlemen were not supposed to comment on a lady's figure. Alice now knew why. His words had sounded seductive and almost carnal. But surely that was due only to his reference to fruit and ripeness and such, she thought a little faintly. Glancing over her shoulder, she saw that her uncle now sat, seemingly forgotten as her mother and Lady Fairley huddled together, some secret satisfaction on their faces. The two were holding a whispered conversation.

"Pray forgive my mother's moodiness," Lord Jonathan murmured, drawing her attention back to him. "We have had a disagreement."

"Oh." Alice seated herself on the bench and proceeded to direct her eyes everywhere but at the huge man settling beside her. It was funny, she hadn't found him particularly threatening upon first seeing him, but he suddenly seemed so . . . male. Embarrassed by her own silliness, she cleared her throat uncomfortably. "I had noticed that she seemed a tad out of sorts."

"Aye."

Alice forced herself to glance at him, only to see that his eyes had gone back to the trio on the opposite bench. Apparently he didn't like what he saw. A small scowl tugged at his features, making his rugged face seem harsher. Surprised, Alice followed his gaze. It seemed Lady Fairley's discussion with Alice's mother was finished, and she and Alice's uncle James were now in the midst of what appeared to be a rather intimate tête-a-tête. Lady Houghton appeared to be dozing in the sun beside them.

"Your uncle . . ." Jonathan asked. His voice was harsh, and Alice turned a questioning glance on him as he continued. "Is he married?"

"Nay. He is widowed. His wife died several years ago, shortly after supplying their only son. He never bothered to remarry."

"Why?"

Alice blinked at the question. The man sounded almost irritated that her uncle hadn't wed again. "Well," she answered slowly, "I suppose his affections were never engaged by any of the eligible widows. And then there was never any apparent need . . . until his son and my father died." She had his full attention at that announcement, and answered his silent question: "They were both taken when the plague struck."

"Ah."

"Aye." She let her breath out on an unhappy sigh, then went on: "Uncle James inherited Father's title and the responsibility for Mother and myself."

"The plague took many," Lord Jonathan said with quiet sympathy. The words made Alice's eyes fill with tears before she could stop them. She had lost a younger sister, her father, her cousin, and her betrothed all in one fell swoop to the plague. The extent of her loss had seemed unbearable at the time. It was still a terrible ache within her. Yet while it was still painful, her anguish had eased a bit with each of the last five years. At times like this, however, the old sorrow caught her by surprise and overwhelmed her. Perhaps that was why she now so loved to lose herself in books, poetry . . .

Embarrassed by her own unexpected display of emotion, Alice glanced away and blinked her eyes rapidly to clear them, wiping surreptitiously at the few small drops that had overflowed to roll down her cheeks.

"What have you done now, Jonathan? You have the poor girl crying."

Alice straightened and shifted to the edge of the bench to make room as Lady Fairley suddenly plopped herself down between them.

"It was nothing he did," she defended quickly. "I was just explaining about my father, sister, cousin, and betrothed all being taken by the plague."

"Oh. Aye. Terrible, that. Jonathan's father, brother, and betrothed were stricken by it as well."

"Oh, dear. I am sorry," Alice murmured.

"Aye. So am I." Lady Fairley's eyes briefly misted over; then determination settled on her face. "In fact, that is the reason we are here at court."

"Is it?" Alice asked politely.

"Aye. Well, 'tis the reason Jonathan is here. I was already here enjoying a nice visit with you and your mother. 'Tis so nice to be able to get out and about after a long, dreary winter like the last."

"Aye," Alice agreed. "'Twas a harsh winter. There was so much snow our men were castle-bound at one point. They had trouble even getting out through the snow to hunt. We were quite desperate for meat."

"We had the same difficulties," Lady Fairley acknowledged solemnly. "That is one of the problems of living in the north."

"Aye."

"I was most eager to get away from Fairley by the time the snow melted. Which is how I happened to be here when Edward sent for Jonathan."

"Oh? The king summoned him here?"

"Aye. I had no idea what it was about, but it turns out that His Highness has decided 'tis time Jonathan weds."

Alice's jaw began to drop; then she caught herself. She couldn't imagine the husky knight being ordered to do anything! "I . . . see," she said finally, at a loss as to what else to say.

"Aye." Lady Fairley heaved a sigh that ended with her glaring at her son. "Jonathan has dallied about the project and the king has run out of patience. He has two weeks to find a bride, else His Highness will find one for him."

"Oh . . . my," Alice said softly, her eyes shooting to Lord Jonathan's face. The man, who'd been silent since his mother's appearance, was looking quite irritated and miserable.

"'Tis quite a fix," Lady Fairley confided unhappily. "Jonathan . . . well, he really is no good at this sort of thing. He prefers jousts and combat. And me, I am of little use. He has already refused to consider every single young woman of marriageable age I have brought before him. I suppose 'tis not surprising. After all, I am an old woman. I hardly know what young people are thinking nowadays, let alone what such young bucks as my son would find attractive."

Alice glanced over at the knight, wondering herself, but he hadn't been paying attention. Without answer, she began, "Oh, aye, well . . ." Lady Fairley suddenly brightened and grabbed Alice's hands. "I have a brilliant idea!"

"You do?" Alice asked warily, suspecting she would not like what was coming.

"You are young and would have a better idea of the kind of bride Jonathan would like. Perhaps you could help him, Alice."

"Me?" She peered at her mother's friend with surprise. This was not something she knew anything about at all!

"Mother," Lord Jonathan suddenly hissed in warning, but the woman ignored him.

"Oh, I do not think—" Alice began.

"'Tis a *fine* idea."

Alice snapped her mouth closed and turned disbelieving eyes to her mother. Lady Houghton was suddenly standing before them, beaming. "Mother—"

"'Twould not be any trouble at all, I am sure, Margaret. Alice would love to help you with your son. Why, she knows plenty of lovely young women for Jonathan to look over. She's been here at court for some time now."

"Look over?" Alice frowned, feeling herself react with indignation at her mother's phrasing. "Rather like looking over falcons, choosing one to hood and bind?" She wanted to be wed someday, but not chosen like property—and she imagined other girls felt the same.

"Aye, it is rather like that, is it not?" Lady Fairley agreed, to Alice's horror.

"Daughter, you can make a list and arrange for Jonathan to meet with those he finds to his taste," Alice's mother enthused.

"'Tis perfect!" Lady Fairley cried, then turned to pat her son's arm soothingly. He looked wary as she said, "You see, dear? With Lady Alice's aid, you should have a bride in no time."

The knight's only answer was a long, drawn-out groan. Alice sympathized.

Chapter Two

"MOTHERS!" WRINKLING HER nose in irritation, Alice waited impatiently for the list she had just finished writing to dry. Thanks to her mother's volunteering her for the task, she had spent the better part of yesterday and most of this morning seeking out the names of every available lady at court—a sorry task, to be sure. There were a dozen other things she would rather have been doing, most of them away from here.

Once, she had been perfectly happy back at Houghton Castle, reading, walking the fields, spending her time in solitary pursuits. Then her mother had begun to worry that she enjoyed her own company too much and insisted on her coming here to London. That had been bad enough in itself—Alice had little patience for the preening and backstabbing she'd discovered went on here at court—but now the dear woman had promised to help her find a bride for Lord Jonathan. Not that it should be so difficult a task. The man was good-looking, strong, and was unquestionably a renowned warrior; the court's ladies would line up to be introduced. But what had possessed her mother to volunteer Alice for this endeavor? Good Lord, her preference for her own company and lack of friendships with other girls her own age had been part of her mother's excuse for bringing her here. How was she now expected to know everyone, and who would be suitable for a man such as Lord Jonathan?

Well, she supposed she had done well enough in making up a list of the available ladies. All it had taken was a little cleverness. Alice had sought out several of the loudest gossips at court and merely mentioned the task she'd been set. Now she had a lovely list. All she had to do was present it to Lord Jonathan and her chore was finished. Just thinking of the man conjured his face, and she found that disturbing. She paused in waving her list to dry it, and contemplated his features in her mind's eye. The man really was quite handsome. And he had been kindness itself yesterday . . . when he hadn't been scowling or frowning at his mother.

She smiled slightly at the memory, then stood. Oddly enough, she had found the scowls endearing. At moments, they had transformed the ragged knight into nothing more than a sulky and suspicious child. And it was clear that the man adored his mother, despite his stormy expressions.

"All finished?"

She glanced up as her mother entered the room. Alice looked at her list. "Aye. You may take it to Lady Fairley now."

"Not I." Her mother smiled. "I have an audience with the queen. You shall have to deliver it. I believe my brother mentioned meeting Lady Fairley and her son in the stables. No doubt you shall find them there if you hurry."

"The stables?" Alice stared at her mother, aghast. "But Uncle has hated horses ever since—"

"Ever since his mount threw him into that tree, breaking his leg," Lady Houghton finished impatiently. "Yes, yes. I have heard that often enough from him. Yet it appears he is willing to visit and perhaps even ride the beasts to please Lady Fairley. Speaking of which, you had best be off before they are away and you miss them."

"Oh, but—" Alice cut off her own protest. Her mother was no longer there to hear it; she had rushed out of the room. Realizing that there was nothing for it but to see to the duty herself. Alice allowed herself a moment of distaste, then quickly rolled up the parchment she held and set off.

Neither Lady Fairley nor Alice's uncle were about, but she did find Lord Jonathan outside the stables. He stood, staring out into the distance, a frown once again clouding his handsome features. Alice paused for a moment to take in his youthful expression, amusement twisting her lips as she gazed upon him. Then, realizing that she was wasting prime reading time—her mother could hardly complain about her loafing around reading if she had an audience with the queen—she took a deep breath, straightened her shoulders, and started forward.

"My lord," she began. "My mother said I might find yourself and Lady Fairley here. Fortune has apparently smiled upon me, for here you are."

The knight glanced around at her words and gave a quick nod. "Aye. Here I am. Unfortunately, my mother is not. She is off on a picnic with your uncle."

"Ah, well . . ." Alice hesitated, as startled by his disgust at that idea as she was by the knowledge itself. Really, she found it difficult to wrap her comprehension around the idea of Lady Fairley being interested in James. The man was a twit. She could not imagine that a woman who had raised such a handsome and strong son as Lord Jonathan would be interested in such a fop.

Pushing the concern aside for later consideration, Alice offered Lord Jonathan a smile. "I suppose it matters little; I can place this in my lord's hands as easily as my lady's."

"What is it?" the big man asked, giving her his full attention as he took the scroll.

"A list of all the eligible ladies presently at court. There are quite a few as you can see."

"Quite a few?" The knight gaped at the list as he unrolled it. "There are at least forty names here." He gave her a pointed look.

"Closer to fifty, actually," Alice agreed, stepping back and preparing to make her escape. "Perhaps you could weed through the names and scratch off those who are obviously unsuitable. Then arrange meetings with the rest and—"

"Brilliant!" Lord Jonathan interrupted. He was looking at her in a way that made her heart flutter. "You and I shall go on a picnic . . . to weed through these names together."

"A picnic?" Alice stared at him blankly. "Oh, I—"

"Well, I hardly know these ladies," he reasoned. "I shall need your assistance in learning of them. And you have proven to be a rather quick girl. Come." Ignoring her weak protests, the big man grabbed Alice's arm and rushed her into the stables. "We must get mounts, but then I know just where we will go."

"BLOODY-MINDED HORSE, BOUNCING me around like a sack of wheat! I swear, my arse is the color of—Oh, I suppose I should not be mentioning such things in your presence, my lady."

Margaret rolled her eyes. James had been complaining since they'd ridden away from the palace into the king's woods, and often with very little concern for the delicacy of his wording. Lady Houghton's brother was rather cruder than she'd expected for a reputed court dandy, and were it possible to use an alternate plan now, she might have considered it. But it was too late for that. Jonathan was already responding beautifully. As she'd expected, her son did not at all care for her recent attentions to James of Houghton. She knew that, as she did for him, her son had very high standards regarding the caliber of anyone she would consider marrying. As if she would ever replace Jonathan's father; what she wanted was grandbabies!

Lady Fairley paused. Looking about, she drew her horse to a halt in a small clearing and dismounted. Waiting until she had both feet planted firmly on the ground, she spoke patiently while removing the two bags she'd attached to her saddle. "I thought we would picnic here. It is as nice a spot as any."

The man stared at her, nonplused for a moment, then gasped. "Good Lord, you don't really intend to picnic, do you?"

"Well, aye, James. 'Twas the idea." Lady Fairley shook her head with amusement. Proceeding to dig out the woolen blanket she'd requested from the king's household for this endeavor, she asked, "Is that a problem?"

"A problem? Of course 'tis a problem!" the old dandy sputtered. "Picnics invite all manner of pests and bug infestations. And there are wild animals out here, Margaret. They will be attracted by the smell, and we shall be forced to fend for our very lives over a scrap of cheese and mutton."

Margaret didn't even bother to roll her eyes at his exaggerated claims; she merely began to lay out the blanket. Calmly she said, "We shall survive, I am sure."

"But—"

"Do you wish to marry your niece off or not?" she interrupted impatiently.

Grimacing, the dandified lord of Houghton grudgingly dismounted.

Lady Fairley nodded with satisfaction as she settled on the blanket. "I thought so."

"Hmm." Lord Houghton's face twisted as he ambled over to where she was now pulling out several items from her bags. He eyed the food greedily, yet still managed to sound irritable as he added, "Aye, of course I want the lass married off. I love my sister and daughter, but Elizabeth has always had a sharp tongue, and Alice has recently shown a distressing tendency to follow in her mother's footsteps. The last thing I need is *two* harping women about!"

Lady Fairley smiled. Betty *had* always been rather sharp-tongued. The woman wasn't a shrew by any means, but she was honest. Especially around those she knew well, she did not curb that honesty with kindness. Her lazy, unambitious brother, who had stumbled into her husband's title, had been the recipient of such treatment on many occasions.

If Alice was showing signs of a similar personality to her mother, it was all as Lady Fairley wished. The last thing she wanted was a sneaky, conniving daughter-in-law. Or a pliant one. She liked to know how things truly lay, and she hoped never to have to wonder with Alice. True, the girl had so far been reserved and quiet, but Margaret believed that was just a show of good breeding. With the right encouragement, the lass would become the brave, thoughtful young woman that Margaret believed would be the only good match for her son. After all, didn't he need someone to challenge him every once in a while, as she herself had done all his life? And a wife needed to be honest, like Alice's mother. And she needed to be someone with enough of a sense of self to be naturally attractive to her son.

A rustling in the bushes caught Lady Fairley's attention, and she glanced into them suspiciously. Her gaze narrowed as she caught a brief glimpse of eyes peering through the branches; then they disappeared.

Aha! she thought with satisfaction. Jonathan had followed . . . as she'd hoped. Also, as she'd expected, he had appeared to be irritated with her choice of companions. *Perfect.* Of course, she'd hoped to have Alice along with her son as well—she'd figured that the best way to get the two together would be to have her son in as many situations with the girl as possible—but everything was a matter of timing, and she would be able to work with this.

Wait! Fate appeared to be smiling on her plans. Margaret was suddenly aware of a light pink cloth showing through the underbrush, and she was fairly certain it was not from anything her son would be wearing.

Turning back to the lunch she had just set out, Lady Fairley murmured under her breath so that only Lord Houghton could hear, "We have visitors."

Much to her amazement, rather than finish sinking down onto the blanket—as he had been doing—the old nobleman straightened and pulled his sword inexpertly from its scabbard. He whirled in place, calling anxiously, "What is it? A wolf? A boar?"

Rolling her eyes at his panicked reaction, Lady Fairley tugged at his breeches. Impatiently she said in a hiss, "Sit down, you old fool. I meant my son and your niece."

Really, she must love her son to be putting up with this clod: Looking slightly embarrassed, Lord Houghton promptly resheathed his sword and settled on the blanket beside her. He grumbled, "Well, you could have just said so."

Her mouth tight with irritation, Margaret tried for a discreet glance toward the bushes, but she couldn't see anything. Hoping that the pair hidden there had missed Houghton's odd behavior, she sought out and found the strawberries. Now she would enact the second part of her plan.

"WHAT ARE WE doing?"

"Shh," Jonathan hissed at Alice, squinting at the pair in the clearing, trying to sort out what was happening. Lord Houghton had jumped up and done a brief spin on the blanket with his sword drawn—as if preparing to fend off a horde of bandits.

Was the old fool trying to impress his mother by acting out made-up tales of bravery? If so, all would be well. Lady Fairley was nothing if not a bright woman, hardly the sort to be impressed by such posturing—especially by such a jester as Lord Houghton. The man was no match for Jonathan's father—now, there had been a true knight and husband!

Reassured, he once more peered through the bushes. His mother was leaning close to the silly Lord Houghton, offering him a strawberry. Oddly, she didn't just hold out the bowl for him to take; she was urging a fruit toward his lips as if he were a babe needing to be coddled.

"What is happening there?" Alice asked impatiently by his ear, making him grimace.

He felt confused himself. "That is what I am trying to figure out! Why is she feeding him like that? Is your uncle so decrepit he cannot feed himself? Must he be fed like a babe?"

Alice moved close enough to peer through the foliage at the couple on the other side. She shrugged impatiently, then said in peevish tones, "She is not feeding him like a babe; she is feeding him like a lover."

"A lover?" He stiffened. "That's impossible. My mother would never do something like that. Besides, I don't see what you mean, anyway."

Alice glanced through the brush again, then looked at him, wide-eyed. "You truly don't see what I mean?" Sighing, she gave an irritated expression he didn't understand, then struggled to her feet. "Wait here."

"What are you doing?"

Alice ignored him and pushed through the bushes out into the clearing. Deaf to his panicky hissed protests, she walked straight over to the couple on the blanket. Smiling at the startled glances her arrival caused, she greeted them cheerfully. "Good day, Uncle, Lady Fairley. I was wondering if I might beg a strawberry from you."

"A strawberry?" they both echoed in bewilderment.

Alice nodded solemnly. "Aye. I wish to show Lord Jonathan something, but I need a strawberry to do it."

"Oh." Lady Fairley and Lord Houghton exchanged a confused glance; then Jonathan's mother reached for the bowl of berries and held them out. "Take as many as you like, dear. We have plenty."

"Thank you." Alice took three and then turned away.

"My dear?" Lady Fairley called.

"Aye?" she asked, turning back.

"Whatever are you *doing* here?" Jonathan thought his mother looked embarrassed.

"Oh, well," Alice explained. "Mother said I should find you by the stables, but instead I found your son. I gave him the list of prospective brides I made up at your request, and he insisted that we come out here for a picnic to look them over."

"A picnic?" Lady Fairley repeated in seeming bemusement. Jonathan felt his annoyance rise.

"Aye." Alice's expression turned confiding. "I fear he neglected to bother to bring the picnic, however."

"Ah." Lady Fairley smiled. "Well, the two of you are more than welcome to join us. We have plenty," she announced.

"I shall be sure to tell your son that," Alice promised. On that note, she whirled away and rushed back through the bushes. As she returned, Jonathan began softly banging his head against a nearby tree trunk. Alice merely arched her eyebrows in response. She shook her head and moved to again sit at his side.

He turned to her at once. "We were supposed to be spying on them—" He broke off abruptly, silenced by a strawberry she popped into his mouth.

"I am aware of that, my lord," she answered as he automatically chewed, then swallowed. "I am not a complete nodcock."

"Well, then why—"

Another berry quieted him.

"Aiding you in finding a bride is one thing," she snapped. "Aiding you to spy on your mother and my uncle in their private moments is quite another. Now . . ."

Alice held a third strawberry out, then smiled in a way Jonathan could only describe as seductive. It was startling enough to make his mouth snap closed. All thoughts of his mother and Lord Houghton disappeared as Alice leaned forward and rubbed the fruit lightly across his lips. "Another succulent, sweet, juicy strawberry, my lord?" she asked.

Jonathan felt his eyes widen incredulously at the girl's husky tone, but his jaws remained stiffly closed. Her perfume was drifting around him, soft and enticing, and he was hard-pressed not to notice the way she was leaning forward, affording him a lovely view down the neckline of her gown. His eyes were drawn devotedly to the soft, luscious mounds of her breasts, which were pressed affectionately together and upward as if ready to leap out of her clothes at him.

As he continued to simply stare at Alice rather dazedly, she drew the berry away from his mouth to her own, luring his gaze to her full, soft, and very kissable lips. He watched her lick very deliberately at the rounded red tip of the fruit and found himself swallowing. Hard. Then she closed her mouth slowly around it. As juice began to run down from one corner of her lips, Jonathan's body tightened in response. His eyes greedily followed the trail that slid down her chin, and he had the sudden insane urge to lean forward and lick it away. Before he could act, though, the girl's own tongue slid out to catch the dripping juice. Jonathan swallowed harshly, aware that his breathing had become fast and heavy; his body was reacting as if she had licked and nipped at him!

Her demonstration apparently over, Alice straightened, her expression promptly becoming businesslike again. She popped the rest of the berry into her mouth and chewed energetically. "You see?" she asked as she swallowed. Her whole demeanor had changed. "Hardly the way one would feed a baby."

Jonathan blinked. He was completely and thoroughly aroused, his body hard and full of desire from her little show. A feeling of frustration overcame him. Worse, he suddenly realized, his mother was feeding that oaf on the other side of the trees in the same way. If it was giving the old man the same ideas it was giving Jonathan—ideas like licking the sticky, sweet juice from Alice's soft lips, pressing her back into the grass and—

He rose to his feet with a roar, drew his sword, then charged through the bushes.

ALICE STARED AFTER Lord Jonathan in amazement, then rushed to her feet and stumbled in pursuit. She reached his side as he paused at the edge of the blanket on which the older couple sat. His hand was clenching his sword, his chest heaving with every breath, and his eyes were darting furiously between his mother and her companion. Those two turned startled gazes up at him.

"Oh, lovely. You decided to join us."

Alice couldn't help but notice that despite the welcome of the words themselves, Lady Fairley sounded far from pleased by Alice and Jonathan's arrival. In fact, the woman was actually glaring at her son. Which was quite odd, Alice decided, since she was sure the invitation earlier had been sincere.

Before she could consider the matter further, Jonathan dropped abruptly onto the edge of the blanket and set his blade down, poking Alice's uncle with its tip in the process. Alice was trying to decide if it had been an accident or not, when the knight reached out to grab her hand and yanked her down, nearly into his lap.

"We are pleased to join you," he claimed, grasping Alice's shoulder to steady her and bestowing an enigmatic smile upon his mother. Then he reached forward, retrieved a strawberry from the small wooden bowl on the blanket, and turned to Alice. "A strawberry, my sweet?" he asked.

"What?" Alice's head shot around to face him, her eyes wide, her mouth gaping slightly. Jonathan popped the berry inside. He then pushed her jaw to chomp on it, before turning to smile at his mother.

"We thought 'twould be nice to enjoy a picnic while we consider my plight."

"Aye. So I heard." Lady Fairley's gaze seemed to narrow on her son with displeasure. "I also hear you forgot the food for this picnic."

"A slight oversight," Jonathan explained through clenched teeth. Then he gave a brilliant smile. "But how is a man expected to think of such petty things with a beauty such as Alice about?"

At that claim Alice's mouth dropped open. She found a second berry popped inside. Jonathan gave her a smile she didn't like and gently pushed her mouth closed. Alice couldn't help it; her eyes narrowed on the big knight suspiciously. Really, it was completely unkind of him to bandy about such compliments when he didn't mean them! Cruel, even. Obviously he had just brought her here as an excuse to spy on his mother!

Swallowing the fruit in her mouth, she turned to speak to Lady Fairley. "Aye, my lady, you understand. Unlike women, 'tis difficult for a man to think of more than one thing at a time. Why, I am constantly amazed that they can walk and converse at the same time. . . . Well, I am amazed by those who can," she added dryly. Turning, she found Jonathan glaring at her. He seemed surprised by her attack. Alice glared right back.

Their staring match was interrupted by what sounded very much like a laugh from Lady Fairley. Alice glanced at the woman, who suddenly burst into a fit of coughs and throat clearing. "Perhaps we should have a look at that list," she suggested after she was through.

Nodding, Alice glanced toward Jonathan expectantly. Scowling and muttering under his breath, the young knight pulled out the scroll he had been given and handed it to his mother. Lady Fairley unfurled the parchment and looked the names over consideringly. "My, 'tis quite a selection, is it not? You are quite fortunate, Jonathan!"

Alice's uncle grunted, leaning over to peer at the list. "Half of them are snaggletoothed hags or harridans. But that still leaves quite a selection."

"Aye." Lady Fairley nodded. "Perhaps we could remove some right now. Shall we go through them?" When no one dissented, she settled more comfortably on the blanket and started to read off names.

Alice sat quietly, listening to the roll of eligible women, but was a bit amazed when Lady Fairley followed each name with a favorable comment. Some of the girls were perfectly lovely, or acceptable in both personality and looks, but really, many of the women Lady Fairley was praising were . . . well . . . *not* praiseworthy. Either Lady Margaret had no clue of the women at court or she simply wanted her son to be married to anyone. While Alice found that a particularly awful concept, she forced herself to keep her thoughts to herself. This was none of her business, after all.

She could stand it no longer, however, when Heloise of Brock's name came up. When Lady Fairley commented that the woman was "such a friendly lass," Alice could not restrain herself. She muttered under her breath, "*Friendly* is right. The girl has been 'friendly' with almost every single one of the king's guards."

Much to Alice's chagrin, despite having simply breathed the comment, Jonathan overheard and gave a guffaw of laughter.

Lady Fairley looked sharply at them. Alice sat up straight, trying to adopt an innocent expression. She suspected she failed miserably. Much to her surprise, it was her uncle who saved her. He nudged Lady Fairley curiously and asked, "Who else is on the list, Margaret?"

Alice saw Jonathan stiffen at Lord Houghton's familiar use of his mother's first name. She sighed inwardly. This was all quite ridiculous.

"Lady Rowena," Lord Jonathan's mother read, then glanced up to smile at them all. "Oh, she is a delightful young girl—such a lovely personality. You really must consider her, Jonathan."

He waited until his mother turned back to the list, then raised an eyebrow in Alice's direction. She hesitated, not wishing to be rude or say anything to draw Lady Fairley's quiet ire again, but really, she decided, it would be too cruel not to give some warning regarding Lady Rowena of Wilcox. The woman was sweet as molasses, but her looks left much to be desired. Rowena weighed as much as Alice's uncle's prize cow, and unfortunately resembled it as well, with large, bovine eyes . . . which were crossed. Giving in to a devilish impulse, Alice nodded, then puffed out her cheeks and crossed her eyes in imitation.

A startled laugh burst from Jonathan's mouth, drawing another sharp glance from his mother. The older woman's eyebrows drew down in definite displeasure. Alice lowered her head repentantly, grateful when Lady Fairley continued.

She had gone through three more names, and was praising Lady Blanche for her gentle kindness, before Alice dared glance up. As she did, Jonathan raised his eyebrows questioningly.

Alice shrugged. She had yet to meet Lady Blanche. Jonathan's response to her signal was to waggle his eyebrows, then jerk his thumb toward himself and nod. Alice took that to mean he *did* know the woman, or at least knew of her. She presumed she was correct when he next sucked his bottom lip and the better part of his jaw back, leaving his top teeth naked and protruding outward, while squinting unattractively in an imitation of the lady in question.

Alice couldn't stop the laugh that spilled from her lips then. It was conjured mostly by how silly he looked. She tried to stop and covered her mouth, her gaze shooting guiltily to Lady Fairley, who'd glanced up again from the scroll.

"Well," the woman said irritably, rerolling the parchment from which she had been reading. "'Tis obvious that we shall not get anything done here today. That being the case, we may as well pack up and head back to the castle. Perhaps you three would be good enough to make a start while I . . . er . . . go for a little walk and clear my head."

Eager to redeem herself, Alice nodded and began to make quick work of the task while Jonathan's mother disappeared. Alice's uncle sat back in a relaxed pose, making it clear he thought this a woman's work. Surprisingly, Lord Jonathan assisted, rewrapping the untouched cheese in its cloth and tossing the unbroken bread in the sack. They were finished quickly and were left to sit and wait on Lady Fairley. She took an inordinate amount of time.

Alice was just thinking the woman might be in distress and need assistance when she suddenly reappeared. Lord Jonathan's mother stumbled out of the woods on the opposite side of the clearing from where she'd entered, looking slightly ruffled and a touch out of breath. Alice noted that with some confusion—she'd assumed the woman had gone on a call of nature—but had little opportunity to comment as the men, apparently more than ready to leave, were immediately up and preparing to do so.

"You know, I believe I have had a wonderful idea," Lady Fairley announced as Jonathan helped Alice refold the blanket upon which they'd sat. "Perhaps we could arrange a dance tonight. Invite all the eligible women. That way, you could make up your own mind as to who is fitting, Jonathan."

Alice glanced at the knight to see how he took the suggestion. She was less than surprised to see it wasn't well. His eyes were wide with what appeared to be horror.

"Mother, may I suggest you not" he began, but Lady Fairley didn't let him get any farther.

"Thank you, son," she said, taking the blanket he held. She slid it quickly back into the bag she had brought, then moved to reattach the bag to her saddle. "Now, you two had best go retrieve your mounts."

Jonathan frowned, then nodded as he watched his mother settle on her horse. "Aye. We shall return directly."

Alice remained silent as he took her arm and led her out of the clearing.

They had tied the steeds some distance from the spot where they had originally come to sit, and Alice realized now that Jonathan had not wanted the horses to alert the older couple to their presence. Of course, she hadn't known what he was up to at the time. He had ridden out hard from the palace, holding on to Alice's reins as if she might turn and ride back if he did not, then had suddenly stopped and cocked his head as if listening. After telling her to wait where she was, he had ridden off, leaving her alone for a few minutes. It was only after he'd reappeared, suggesting she dismount and proceeding to tie the horses to a tree branch, that he'd let her accompany him farther. He'd led her off through the bushes then to the spot he'd chosen from which to spy.

Alice's honest nature had balked at the infringement of their family members' privacy as soon as she'd realized Lord Jonathan's intent. In fact, she had been looking for an excuse to let the couple know of their presence when she rushed in to borrow the strawberries. Well, that, and she'd suddenly given in to a desire to see what Lord Jonathan would look like while she was feeding him.

At any rate, the upshot of their actions was that they had a bit of a walk before they reached the horses . . . or, to be more exact, *Jonathan's* horse. Her own appeared to be missing.

"What the devil?" Spotting the lone animal, Jonathan rushed forward through the trees. Alice was hard on his heels. Reaching his mount, the big man looked it over, then examined the branch where the stallion's reins were still tied. "Damn! Someone has stolen your horse."

"Do you really think so?" Alice glanced around nervously. "Perhaps he merely came untied and wandered off."

"Nay. I tied him well. I was sure to tie them both well." Jonathan freed his mount, scowling around the area. "Someone has to have taken yours."

"Oh, dear." She glanced around the woods to the tree where her horse had been tied. "Well . . ." She brightened.

"I can ride back with my uncle. They are waiting in the clearing, after all."

"Aye." Giving a nod, Jonathan put a foot in the stirrups of his horse. Alice turned to start back through the woods, but then she heard him call.

"What are you doing?"

Glancing back over her shoulder, she answered, "Heading back to the clearing to—" Her words were cut off as her foot was caught on a branch that sent her tumbling. Embarrassed and muttering, she quickly started to push herself onto her knees, then froze at the sight of a bit of blue cloth snagged on a branch near her face. It was the same blue as Lady Fairley's gown. A moment later she was caught under the arms and lifted unceremoniously to her feet.

"Are you all right?"

Alice glanced up in surprise at the concern in Lord Jonathan's voice. He wasn't looking at her; his gaze was traveling down her body in the wake of his hands as he checked her over to be sure she wasn't injured. She flushed at the familiar way his fingers skimmed over her, and took a quick step back, nearly tumbling again.

"I am fi-fine," she got out a little breathlessly as he caught her arms to steady her. "Really," Alice added when he continued to look concerned. After a brief pause, he swallowed and nodded, then turned to grab at the reins of his mount.

Her gaze moved distractedly back to the small swatch of blue cloth on the ground by her feet. She was about to draw Jonathan's attention to it, when she was suddenly caught by the waist and lifted onto his horse.

Alice promptly began to protest. "Oh, really, my lord. There is no need for us to ride. I can walk back to the clearing. I—"

At last she gave up her protests, mostly because he was ignoring her. He mounted in front of her and drew her hands around his waist.

"Hold on," he instructed.

Alice nodded against his back, breathing in deeply to try to steady her nerves. It was rather novel to be in such close proximity to a man. She had never done so before. Unmarried women were simply not allowed such familiarity. Of course, this was an unusual circumstance, and . . .

Her thoughts died as she breathed in the scent of him. He smelled of the woods and the river and . . . male. It was a surprisingly pleasant mix, she decided, breathing it in again as her fingers interlocked at his middle. Feeling the muscles of his stomach bunch and ripple, she flattened her fingers over them to get the full sensation, then, realizing what she was doing, stopped breathing in embarrassment. Her fingers stilled.

Of course, Alice couldn't go long holding her breath. She managed to do so for the short ride back to the clearing, but there the breath left her in a slow hiss. The place was empty. Lady Fairley and her uncle had not waited for them; they had apparently ridden on ahead. Alice recalled the small swatch of cloth she had spotted near the horses and pondered silently, wondering why Lady Fairley had been by the horses. Surely *she* hadn't untied Alice's mount and let it go? Had she really been so annoyed with Alice as to wish to have her walk back to the castle?

"Well, we shall have to ride quickly to catch up," Lord Jonathan said.

Alice glanced at the back of his head, then pressed close and held on tightly as he spurred his mount into a trot. She didn't hold her breath this time. Instead she sat, her breasts pressed against his back, her hands clutched at his front, breathing in deeply of his scent.

She was enjoying it so much, it took her most of the ride to realize that despite his words, Jonathan wasn't trying very hard to catch up to her uncle and his mother. He had the horse going at a trot, but a rather slow one, really. They had ridden here faster. She was so startled by the realization that she loosened her hold and started to pull away, but he stopped her by catching her hands with one of his own.

"You had best hold on," he said. "I would not wish to see you fall."

Alice wondered at the husky note to his voice, but decided to merely enjoy the ride. She relaxed against him.

Chapter Three

JONATHAN MANAGED TO keep his smile in place as his toes were trampled by yet another dance partner, but only just. He could honestly say that even the siege of Calais, where he had suffered a wound to the stomach that had caused him immeasurable pain and nearly killed him, was preferable to this hell his mother had arranged.

His bridal feast. That was what she called it. She had arranged for the celebration with the king, and now Jonathan was suffering through it. His first complaint was with the name. Shouldn't it be called the groom's feast? It was *his* feast, and *he* was the proposed groom, after all. Yet nay; his mother claimed it was to find him a bride; therefore it was his bridal feast.

Jonathan's face twisted with disgust. As silly as the name was, the actual event itself was worse. His mother had managed to finagle the use of the great hall in the palace. The king and queen were in attendance.

Jonathan's eyes slid unhappily to the glowering monarch and his wife. Edward had been sternly glaring, mostly at Jonathan, since arriving. He supposed it was to show how seriously His Majesty meant his orders to be taken. Jonathan was getting the message.

Another stomp on his toe drew his attention back to his dance partner. He sighed inwardly. The woman was myopic and a venerable four-and-thirty. Jonathan was thirty, himself, and so he supposed she was not *that* old—but she was well past the age considered prime for childbearing. She should have been crossed off the list at the picnic, but, in the end, no one had been crossed off that list. His mother had left the whole thing intact. Every woman at court was in attendance here tonight.

Looking around, Jonathan found his thoughts wandering to Alice and their ride back to the castle two days earlier. He instinctively sought the Houghton girl out where she stood with her mother, her uncle, and his own mother near the king and queen.

Much to Jonathan's surprise, he had found himself preoccupied with thoughts of the lass ever since that day. And not just any thoughts. He kept recalling her husky voice as she'd pressed that cool, sweet strawberry to his lips, could still smell the scent that had drifted off of her, ensnaring him in its erotic spell. And the vision he'd glimpsed of her delectable breasts, too, they kept rising before his eyes, blinding him to all else around him. Then, there were his sensual memories from their return trip that haunted him. If he concentrated, Jonathan would swear he could still feel her arms around his body and her breasts pressed against his back.

Yes, he had found himself undoubtedly aroused by that ride. His body had reacted to this girl as it had to no other, and that very fact had left him somewhat embarrassed and discomfited once they reached the stables. Jonathan had found himself avoiding Alice's gaze, as if she might read the less-than-sterling thoughts that had been tumbling through his mind. So he had done a fine job of avoiding her ever since.

It hadn't been difficult, he thought with sudden annoyance. The girl had hardly sought him out.

Another crunch of his toes drew Jonathan's attention back to the reel. Fortunately, the musicians ended the song, saving his dance partner from his exasperation. Gritting his teeth, he walked the lady back to her mother, then glanced around the waiting horde with a sigh. There were countless women in this room, and three men. Two, he corrected himself as his gaze slid to where the king had been standing just moments before. Having done his duty by making an appearance, Edward and his wife had apparently taken themselves off to more amusing entertainments than watching the Scourge of Crécy dance with more willing damsels than there'd been French at that victory.

Scowling at the thought, Jonathan let his gaze roam to Lord Houghton. As the only other man present, the old bugger might have lent some assistance with this mob, he thought with resentment. Instead, the velvet-clad old fop appeared glued to his mother's side. Houghton had been hovering over Lady Fairley all night, leaving Jonathan to usher snaggletoothed female after nasty old crone onto the dance floor under the watchful gaze of some fifty want-to-be brides and their mamas, aunts, and other chaperones.

The two times he had dared beg for rest, returning to the trestle tables for his ale mug, he had found himself surrounded by that crowd of she-wolves. Subjected to their titterings and twitterings as they bombarded him with long, lavish dissertations on their skill at embroidery and such, despite his sore feet, Jonathan had quickly resorted each time to dancing again, simply to get away.

Becoming aware that his partnerless state was once again making him a target, and that the maternal swarm was closing in, Jonathan murmured his excuses to the nearest she-wolves and swiftly made his way to where his own mother, Alice, her uncle, and Lady Houghton stood. "Mother, may I—"

"Ah, Jonathan!" his mother interrupted gaily. "This is a wonderful success, do you not think?"

"Nay, I *do not* think," he snapped, which, wiped the self-satisfied expression off her face.

"What?" she asked in injured tones. "But it is working beautifully."

"Nay. It is working horribly," he corrected.

"But—"

"Mother, there are at least one hundred and fifty women here."

"Well, aye," she agreed soothingly. "But only fifty of them are really of any concern; the rest are merely here to chaperon the girls."

"Still, fifty women and one man are not exactly even odds, are they?"

"Oh, Jonathan," she pshawed. "You are a warrior. Surely you can handle this gaggle of females. Besides, you are not the only man here; Lord Houghton is in attendance." She pointed that out and moved closer to the man, running her hand down his arm in a possessive manner that made Jonathan's skin crawl.

Jonathan snapped, "Well, he may as well not be for all the good he is doing."

"Jonathan!" Lady Fairley turned, obviously shocked by her son's bad manners.

He was beyond tact. "Do not 'Jonathan' me. Lord Houghton has been standing here slobbering over you all evening while I have had my feet danced off, my toes crushed, my ears talked away, my best tunic stained by several clumsy wenches too busy blabbing to watch where they were going, and . . ." He paused to sniff experimentally in Alice's direction, then said in a snarl, "And damned if my sense of smell has not been ruined by the rank bodies or overindulgence in perfume by half of the noblewomen of London!"

ALICE BIT HER lip at Lord Jonathan's outburst, her urge to laugh nearly overwhelming her. She peered curiously at Lady Fairley to see what the woman's reaction to this would be. Margaret of Fairley stood for a moment, mouth agape; then, much to Alice's amazement, her face crumpled like a child's.

"You never appreciate *anything* I do for you, Jonathan. Here I worked so hard at getting permission to hold a feast for you—you know the king feels indebted to you if he'll arrange for this—then attaining the room, arranging the food and drink and inviting everyone, and all you can do is—"

"Oh, I am sure your son appreciates your efforts, my lady," Alice found herself stepping in to say. Guilt had washed over the man's face. "I think he is merely stating that he is a bit overwhelmed. Perhaps 'tis expecting a lot from him to entertain so many women at once. Mayhap 'twould have been better had you invited some men to help with this endeavor."

"Exactly," Lord Jonathan said. "Finally, a woman with some sense."

"Are you suggesting that I have no sense?" Lady Fairley asked with icy politeness. Alice nearly laughed aloud at the poleaxed look on the knight's face.

"Nay, nay," he began quickly. "Of course not, Mother. I never meant to suggest—"

When Lady Fairley opened her mouth in what Alice suspected would be a furious blasting, she couldn't stop herself from intervening again. "I am sure he meant no insult, my lady. It is obvious he is quite worn out from doing his duty this evening and is not thinking straight. Perhaps it would be best if he were to take a stroll in the night air and let his thoughts clear."

"Aye." Jonathan leaped at the proffered escape. Yet, rather than simply slipping away, as she expected, he latched on to her hand and drew her with him. "A little walk through the gardens will be of great assistance in reviving me."

"Oh, but I do not—" Alice protested as he drew her away from the great hall.

"Come. Your presence will keep those other women from following to harass me," he insisted.

As he pulled her along behind him, Alice made a face at his back, but there seemed little use in arguing. Besides, she too was quite ready to get out of the feast. This had been a terribly boring evening for her; standing on the sidelines, watching Jonathan dance with a multitude of ladies. The entire time she was recalling how it had felt to be pressed close to his body, and the scent of him as they had ridden back to court after the picnic.

Alice sighed as those memories enveloped her again. They had a nasty tendency of doing so these last two days, and she didn't at all understand why. She had never before had such problems, never before been plagued by the memory of any single event, but it seemed these days her mind was constantly full of Jonathan and their time together.

"Thank the Lord."

Alice was drawn from her thoughts to find that they had finally made their way outside. Falling into step beside him, she breathed in deeply of the night air and felt herself relax. It was only then that she realized she had been rather stiff and tense all evening. She'd found it irritating to watch Jonathan trip about with all his whirling maidens. Some part of her had even thought it terribly unfair that he hadn't asked her to dance, at least *once.* . . .

Just so she could compare it to how it felt to hold him on horseback, she assured herself quickly. But Alice knew that wasn't true. A part of her was quite unhappy that she wasn't under consideration to be Lord Jonathan's bride, and she couldn't help but wonder why. Not to mention that she couldn't understand why his mother seemed to like her fine when Jonathan wasn't around but showed definite signs of annoyance whenever he was in her company.

"Watch your step."

Alice jerked her attention back to where she was walking, just barely managing to avoid stepping in a dark mass of something unpleasant.

"Where are we going?" She glanced around a bit anxiously. Normally she would not be alone like this with a man. Even the son of a family friend. Actually, now that she thought of it, she was flummoxed that her mother wasn't trailing behind, acting as chaperon. Glancing over her shoulder she saw that no, there was no one following, and yes, they were definitely alone. Most unusual, she decided with confusion.

"The stables."

Alice turned her attention forward again at that answer.

"Why?"

"I thought we might go for a ride."

Alice brightened at the thought—sitting behind him again, her arms around him, their bodies pressed close together—then caught back her enthusiasm. Firstly, he likely intended her to be on her own mount. Second, it was not very safe to ride at night. A horse could easily make a misstep and be injured. Also, this simply was not a good idea. What if someone caught them out here? What would people think of her virtue?

Sensing her resistance, and that this time it was a true resistance, Lord Jonathan paused to glance back at her. Her solemn expression seemed to jog his memory about propriety, and he sighed unhappily. "I suppose a ride is out of the question."

"Aye," Alice quietly agreed.

He nodded in resignation. "I just thought it would be nice to ride with you again. I enjoyed it the other day."

Alice blinked at that awkward admission. He wasn't looking at her when he said it; his gaze actually danced everywhere but on her, still, it took her a moment to recognize his sudden shyness, and to realize that he was sincere in his claim. He had enjoyed their ride as much as she had!

"Perhaps . . ." she began, then paused. He was finally looking at her, and his gaze was trained on her mouth. It caused an odd tingling to start in her lips, and breathlessness overcame her. She could not have spoken had she wished. When he started to sway nearer, Alice felt her ability to breathe evaporate altogether. She was absolutely, positively certain he was about to kiss her. She allowed herself to sway toward him in response.

"Jonathan! Oh, there you are! I told James I thought you had gone this way."

Alice and Jonathan leaped guiltily apart and swung around. Lady Fairley and Alice's uncle were approaching through the darkness.

"Mother." The word was almost a groan on Jonathan's lips. Alice could sympathize completely. She felt rather like making a similar noise herself at the moment. His mouth had been so close to hers that she had felt his breath on her tender, tingling lips. But that promise was apparently not to be fulfilled tonight.

"I have decided to forgive you," Lady Fairley announced. She reached them and slid her arm through her son's. "In fact, I have decided you may even be somewhat . . . well, not *completely* wrong about tonight's endeavor."

"Oh?" The knight definitely sounded wary, Alice thought distractedly. Her uncle silently drew her hand onto his arm and they followed Lady Fairley and her son back from the stables.

"Aye," Alice heard Margaret say. "In fact, I have decided to have another feast."

"Another one?" Lord Jonathan came to an abrupt halt.

"Aye. Another one." His mother laughed at his obvious horror and drew his arm back under hers to drag him along. She added gaily, "Two, in fact. Now I just have to speak to the king."

WHILE JONATHAN HAD spent the two days between the picnic and yestereve's feast avoiding Alice and the confusing feelings she stirred in him, the first thing he did upon awakening this morning was to go in search of her. He found the girl breaking her fast in the great hall, where it appeared almost every other guest at court was also eating. The room was overflowing with people, and the benches groaned under the weight of their numbers.

Alice sat at one of the upper tables, her mother on one side, a leering ogre Jonathan didn't know on her other. Striding forward, he managed, with a scowl and an elbow, to make the fellow, one who sat entirely too close to Alice, shift over enough to allow him to squeeze between them.

Alice twisted on the bench in surprise as he unintentionally jostled and nudged her, trying to claim the small space available. Much to his pleasure, the action left her chest smashed against his. Jonathan found himself quite enjoying the situation for the few seconds it lasted, then the girl blushed bright pink and turned to face forward again.

"Good morn, my lord," she said.

Jonathan smiled at the strangled sound of her voice, knowing she was embarrassed. He also knew that his own voice would come out similarly at the moment if he used it—but not from embarrassment. The brief and intimate contact of their bodies had left him almost instantly aroused. Clearing his throat, he grunted in greeting and concentrated on the food and drink set before him. He allowed his body to recover before turning his attention again to her.

Those few moments allowed her to recover her composure, he saw. The red had receded from her face, and a slightly dreamy expression had replaced the embarrassed look of only moments before. "Do you have any plans for the day, my lady?" he asked.

"Nay. Why do you ask, my lord?" She glanced at him curiously, then, as he shuffled through his mind for an answer that eluded him, understanding came to her face. A crooked smiled claimed her lips. "Oh, of course. The list."

"The list?" Jonathan repeated blankly.

"Aye. No doubt you wish to go over the list again . . . now that you have interacted with some of those on it. So that you may cross off those you found unacceptable," she added when he continued to stare blankly at her.

"Ah, yes," he murmured. His eyes fell back to his trencher as he contemplated that. It hadn't really been why he'd sought her out this morning. He couldn't say why he had; he'd simply wanted to see her. He had been pondering kissing her since his mother had interrupted what he was pretty sure would have been a hell of a kiss. Of course, he couldn't be positive he would have kissed her. He hadn't really been thinking at that point. At least, he hadn't been thinking, *I am going to kiss her.* Mostly he had been thinking that her lips looked full and soft and tempting, and that they probably tasted as good as they looked, and—

Well, this is neither here nor there, Jonathan told himself. The point was, he had spent a good half of last night imagining a kiss he hadn't given her. The other half *had been spent* dreaming that he *had* kissed her . . . and more. He'd had terribly lascivious dreams, full of Alice's naked, creamy flesh in his hands and mouth, enclosing his hard—

"I had no plans for the day and would be pleased to assist you in this matter."

For a moment, Jonathan thought she meant in the matter he had dreamed of. His heart nearly leaped through his chest with gratitude at the thought, and his body instantly became hard again. He gave his head a shake, peered at her innocent, smiling face, then realized she must mean she would be happy to go over her list with him.

It hadn't at all been the reason he'd sought her out, but he supposed it was the reason he *should* have sought her out.

"Wonderful," he said, frowning at the huskiness of his voice. Clearing his throat, he tried again. "That would be very helpful, thank you."

"If you are through breaking your fast, we may even do so now." Much to Jonathan's horror, she actually started to rise. Grabbing her arm, he stopped her when she would have moved away from the table.

"I, er . . ." He peered down at his lap briefly, then realized that the action was likely to draw her attention to the unfortunate state of his manhood. He raised his gaze abruptly. Clearing his throat, he murmured, "I am not through eating."

When her gaze moved with confusion to his trencher, Jonathan noticed that he had absently consumed every last bite of food that had been set before him.

"I am oddly ravenous this morn," he explained lamely, but she nodded and relaxed back into her seat. Breathing a sigh of relief, Jonathan gestured a servant over and requested more food and another drink. He then glanced at Alice with a smile. Noting the sidelong looks being shot at the two of them by Alice's mother, Jonathan leaned forward and said, "I trust you are feeling well this mom, my lady?"

"Oh." Lady Elizabeth of Houghton flushed. "Aye. Thank you, my lord. And you? Are you prepared for the day's endeavors?"

"Endeavors?" he asked cautiously.

"Aye. Preparations for your next feast."

"What?" Jonathan had no qualms about letting his horror show. Another feast? Over his dead body! He would never again willingly suffer the tortures he had experienced the evening before. He had only refrained from arguing last night because he'd assumed the king would never agree to such activities in his palace. It seemed his mother had more persuasive power with Edward than he'd imagined.

"Oh, dear." Alice's murmur drew his questioning gaze, and she explained, "I had quite forgotten about the feasts. I promised this morning to assist your mother with the preparations."

"That is unnecessary," he said. "I really do not think that another event will be necessary. The last, while not completely unhelpful, was something of an ordeal I would rather not see repeated."

"Oh, but that is why I agreed to assist. I wanted to be sure that it would not be another like last night's debacle," she explained earnestly. "This time, only appropriate women shall be invited. And half of the attendees shall be men, to help balance things out. This way, the other men may entertain the others while you concentrate on one lady at a time. You see?" She smiled at him brightly. "I am sure it will work out much better."

Jonathan grimaced. He was not reassured by the news, but it seemed he had little choice in the matter. Worse, it appeared that Alice was now throwing herself into helping his mother find him a bride.

Now, why did that idea annoy him so much?

Chapter Four

"Oh, I AM so sorry, my lord. I am so clumsy."

"What? Oh." Jonathan tore his gaze away from Alice to force a smile for the young woman with whom he was dancing. The throbbing in his toes told him she was apologizing for stomping on his foot. It was the first time Jonathan had been so stomped all evening, but he had hardly noticed the action. His attention had been riveted on Lady Houghton's daughter—and the man presently leading her across the dance floor.

Damn his mother and her never-ending plans! he thought irritably. Muttering some polite comment about his dance partner's misstep, he turned his gaze back to Alice. This was the second bridal feast—the result of several days of work carried out by his mother, himself, Alice, and her mother. Lord Houghton had been present, as well, but that was all. The man was a layabout who apparently considered any manual labor to be beneath him.

Jonathan sighed inwardly. Normally there were a thousand and one other things he would rather have done with the last few days. Certainly bickering over what food and drink to serve at these bloody feasts his mother kept planning was ludicrous for a warrior such as himself. However, none of his alternate pastimes would have included Alice's presence. She had pledged to assist his mother, and that meant that, for him to spend time around her, he'd had to assist as well. And Jonathan had found himself hungering for Alice's presence.

Actually, the lass had managed to make the past two days fun. She and Jonathan had talked and laughed their way through his mother's orders, enjoying each other's company and working together. As he'd suspected, Alice was a clever woman, and her witty turn of phrase and irreverent sense of humor drew Jonathan like a moth to a flame. He only hoped he did not get burned.

"Oops. I have done it again."

This time Jonathan did not need to be told, he'd definitely felt the crunching of his toes as the reel brought him and his partner together again. Had it been a deliberate stomp, with a twist at the end to inflict the most damage? It did not take a lot of thought to realize that the delicate little brat he was dancing with was annoyed with his lack of attention.

He would have been enraged once, but Jonathan was honest enough to admit that he *was* being rude in his lack of attention. He likely even deserved his dance partner's attacks, petty as they were. In truth, he had been rude to almost every single maid he had danced with, what with his gaze and attention being taken up as they were by Alice and her suitors. The wench had hardly sat a dance out. She was forever fluttering around the floor on the arm of one lordling or another. Why the hell had he allowed his mother to invite so many damned men? he wondered irritably. And did they all have to be so bloody attractive?

The third stomp was the final one Jonathan was willing to suffer. It was also the most painful of the three and left him limping as he escorted the little brat off the floor. Leaving her to complain of his distraction to her mama, Jonathan sought out his own mother, intending to do a little complaining of his own.

"Ah, there is my handsome son."

Jonathan grimaced inwardly at his mother's words as he paused at her side, but he gave a polite nod to the group of noblewomen gathered about Lady Fairley. He was beginning to feel like the pride of a stable, being presented for possible stud service.

"Here you are, my dear."

Jonathan did grimace openly as the ever-present Lord Houghton appeared with a drink for his mother, but in truth, it was more from habit than anything else. It was now clear the man was nothing more than a nuisance. Jonathan was positive his mother had more sense than to do aught but dally with the oaf's affections. Of course, if she suddenly decided to marry the bastard, Jonathan would have to kill him, but he would worry about that when and if the time came. At the moment, he was more concerned with Alice's antics.

"My, this was a brilliant idea, Jonathan, and a fine success. Do you not think?"

He nodded absently, hardly hearing his mother's question or the cooed agreement of the surrounding women. He irritably watched yet another man lead Alice through a reel. She was a graceful dancer, her body perfectly in tune to the music. She put all the others to shame.

"Do you not think so, Jonathan?" his mother asked again.

"Hmm?" He glanced around to find a dozen expectant faces turned toward him. He nodded distractedly, then commented, "Lady Alice appears to be quite popular, does she not? She has danced with nearly every man here."

His mother waved that away impatiently. "Really, Jonathan. Whatever does it matter whom Lady Houghton is dancing with? She is not the one who needs to marry. You are. Now, why do you not give Lady Jovell a turn on the floor? You have not danced with her yet."

Jonathan frowned at the suggestion, but he was too polite to give any insult by refusing. He took the arm of the spotty-faced girl who stepped out of the group and led her onto the floor. Fortunately, the chit was the quiet sort who did not seem to desire conversation while dancing. She also didn't seem to mind that his gaze was trained on Lady Alice and the bevy of beaux vying to dance with her. Of course, that may only have been because she spent the entire dance with her head bowed, watching her feet.

At least she did not treat him to a sound foot-stomping for his inattention, and that was something to recommend her, he decided as the music finally ceased.

Afraid that his mother might try to push another young maid on him, Jonathan made returning Lady Jovell a quick business. He merely escorted her back to the group around Lady Fairley, then hurried away, pretending he did not hear his mother when she called.

He moved off in such a rush that he nearly ran over Alice. Steadying her with a hand, he beamed brightly, his first real smile of the night, and promptly took her arm.

"Ah, there you are. Come. Dance with me."

"Come here, come there, come dance with me," Alice muttered, and Jonathan glanced down at her with concern. There was an opening on the dance floor, but he paused, facing her, to await the music.

"Do you not wish to dance with me?"

"Oh." She smiled wryly. "It is not that, my lord. Although I am a bit winded and was hoping for a chance to rest."

"Then what—"

"You have a tendency to order me about, my lord," she pointed out dryly. "Rather like a lackey. And while I realize that I agreed to assist you, I had not realized that it was to be in such a subservient position."

"Subservient?" The expression he gave her was aghast. "I hardly look upon you as a servant."

"Nay?" She raised an eyebrow, a wry smile tugging at her lips. "'Tis my error, then."

The music began, and they both fell silent as the dance started. The steps first distracted, then separated them as they hopped and skipped through several partners.

The moment they were back together, Jonathan cleared his throat and said, "You said you were hoping to rest. Would you prefer—"

"Nay. I am fine, my lord. I may rest after this dance."

"Ah. I am not surprised that you are weary. I had noticed that you appear to be quite popular as a dance partner."

Jonathan wished he could retract the words the moment they left his mouth. The comment had definitely sounded rather peevish, and the curious look Alice sent him before the steps of the dance drew her away from him again made clear that she had taken notice of it. It seemed an eternity before the dance returned her to him.

"I was rather amazed myself at my popularity," was her mild comment as they moved together through a simple alman.

"Amazed?" He scowled at her. "There is nothing to be amazed about. You are a beautiful woman, intelligent and witty. Of course you are popular." He did not sound pleased by this admission, even to himself.

"Do you really think so?"

Jonathan glanced down sharply at her almost whispered query. The girl's eyes had gone all soft and dewy. For a moment he was positive that she might cry just from his giving her such a compliment; then he spared the time to toss another glare in her uncle's direction. Obviously the wretch did not waste time complimenting Alice as he should. As anyone who loved her—and in whose care she had been left—should do.

"Aye," he said quietly. "I think you are all those things and more, Alice."

"Do you think we might slip outside for another walk?" she asked.

Jonathan blinked in surprise, his mind suddenly awhirl with possibilities. A romantic walk under the stars? A chance to claim that kiss he had missed out on two nights before? Then he noted Alice's expression as she apparently realized just what she had suggested. Fearing she might retract the offer, he headed quickly for the door.

They were just about to slip out when his mother and Alice's suddenly stepped into their path.

"*There* you are!"

Jonathan closed his eyes. He was becoming heartily sick of that phrase.

"Alice, your mother is not feeling well, and she would like you to accompany her back to your room."

Jonathan wasn't at all fooled by the claim. He could clearly see the determination in his mother's eyes. He had also taken notice of the startled expression on Lady Houghton's face before she managed to cover it with what he supposed she believed could pass for the pathetic expression of an ailing individual.

"Oh, Mother!" Alice was immediately at the older woman's side, offering her arm for support. "Is it something you ate, do you think?"

"I, er, I am not sure, dear." Lady Houghton's gaze jumped to Lady Fairley, then away. "It may be. I simply feel awful."

Lady Houghton was a lousy thespian, Jonathan decided. He sighed unhappily as his chance to get Alice outside, alone under the moon and stars, slipped away.

"Well, come, we shall get you above stairs and put you to bed." Casting a regretful glance in Jonathan's direction, Alice departed with her mother, leaving Jonathan to turn an irritated glance on his own. Before he could catapult the accusations swimming around in his head, however, she drew forward a young stick like figure in a dress and smiled brilliantly. "This is Lady Estemia Kolpepper, my dear. You have not yet had the chance to dance with her."

Outmaneuvered again, Jonathan gave his mother a look that promised retribution and took the arm of his latest offering.

JONATHAN WAS HEARTILY sick of seeing Alice fly by on the arm of some man or other. It did not matter that he himself had danced with equally as many women. The fact was, she was far too popular with the men in attendance at this, his last day of bridal feasting, and he did not like it.

The dance finally ended and Jonathan escorted his latest partner off the floor. He left her in the general vicinity of where he had collected her, then strode purposely toward Alice. He'd had quite enough of dancing with clumsy oxen and spoiled mama's girls. Jonathan had also had quite enough of watching Alice dragged across the floor by every lecher at court. Had his mother deliberately invited every ne'er-do-well who gathered around the king?

"Oh, Jonathan." Alice beamed on him when he paused before her. "Have you met Lord Roderic of Somersby?"

"Nay, and I do not wish to," was his abrupt answer. He swept her out onto the dance floor as the musicians started again.

The first song had ended and a second begun before he noticed the way Alice was shaking silently at his side. For a moment, his black mood was displaced by concern that she might be crying or some such womanly thing, but then he glimpsed the expression on her face. It was mirth she was attempting to subdue that was making her shake so.

"What the devil do you find so amusing?" he asked.

"You," she answered promptly, a laugh slipping out before she could stop it. "You look like a sulky boy. What has gotten under your cap, my lord? Not enjoying this bridal feast?"

Jonathan growled at her gentle teasing, his gaze moving hungrily over her sparkling eyes and cheerful grin. "No, but I notice *you* have been enjoying it."

"If you think so, my lord, I fear you are sadly mistaken." She spoke so cheerfully, for a moment Jonathan wasn't sure he had heard right.

"Are you saying you are not enjoying the feast?"

Her smile slipped and she sighed. "My lord, my feet ache, it is positively stifling in here, and if I have to listen to one more grand tale of bravery in battle, I shall surely die of boredom."

For some reason, her litany of miseries cheered Jonathan somewhat. He found himself smiling at her in return.

"My lord, are you aware that the music has changed again?" When he stared at her blankly, she explained, "This is our third reel."

"I had not noticed," Jonathan admitted wryly. "After three days of feasting and dancing, all the songs are sounding the same." He leaned forward and confided, "I have been judging the length of a dance by how many times my feet were stepped on."

ALICE WAS AMUSED by Lord Jonathan's admission, but the man had obviously not taken her point. "Well, I fear your mother has noticed even if you have not, and she appears to be growing irritated."

Her dance partner glanced over toward his mother, but his only reaction was to tighten his hand on hers.

She decided to try again. "In fact, she is beginning to look quite vexed. Really, my lord, I take her point. Is this feast not about finding a bride for you? 'Twill be difficult for you to do so should you continue dancing with me, neglecting the women brought here for you to consider."

"I need consider the matter no further. Any one of them is interchangeable with the others. Besides, I like dancing with *you*. You do not step on my toes, you do not breathe garlic into my face, you do not spill food on me, and you can converse."

Alice blinked once, twice, then ventured, "Converse? I take it you have found some of the women—"

"Unable to string two words together that have more than four letters in them. And many of them are deceitful. You should hear what they say about each other!"

"Oh, dear." Alice bit her tongue to keep from laughing. Then she became worried. "Oh, my. Your mother is headed in our direction. I suspect she is about to tell you that you should be dancing with the others."

Lord Jonathan glanced over his shoulder, his expression becoming irritated. He promptly began to walk Alice in the opposite direction.

"What are you doing?" she asked in surprise.

"I am getting us out of here."

"Oh, but—" Alice began. She got no farther as Lord Jonathan picked up the pace. He hustled her out of the great hall, and a glance over Alice's shoulder just before they slipped through the door showed Lady Fairley pausing, hands on hips, eyes narrowed, as she watched them flee. She did not look at all pleased. Once again, Alice was reminded that the woman positively did not see her as bridal material for her son. She found herself inexplicably saddened.

Lord Jonathan slowed to a walk once they were outside, and Alice glanced at him curiously, peering at his face in the moonlight. His distraction was obvious, so she left him to his thoughts and they walked in companionable silence for several moments; then she recognized the path he had taken. She smiled slightly.

"The stables again, my lord?" she asked with quiet humor.

"What?" He sounded bewildered, then glanced around and seemed to realize she meant their destination. He shook his head. "Nay."

Despite his negation, they continued silently in that general direction, but Alice didn't question him further. She noted, however, that he was rubbing his stomach absently, his gaze and face working as if he were resolving some problem. Quite suddenly he asked, "Are you hungry, Alice?"

Startled by his use of her given name, it took Alice a moment to digest his question. She considered it seriously and nodded with some surprise. "Aye. Actually, I am."

"As am I. Come." Taking her hand again, he tugged her off the path they had been on and along another, this one leading around the back of the keep. He urged her silently through a door there, pressed a finger to his lips, then led her along a dim hallway that grew warmer as they went.

"Wait here," he instructed, bringing her to a halt outside a set of double doors. He slid through.

Alice obeyed for all of a minute; then curiosity got the better of her. She cautiously eased open the door, and wasn't at all surprised to see that the doors led into the kitchens. And what a huge kitchen it was, she thought with awe. Houghton Castle had a rather large scullery of its own, but this had to be at least ten times bigger. Alice supposed that it was necessary here at the palace. Certainly Houghton Castle, even with all its servants and men-at-arms, still had nowhere near the number of people to feed as did the palace.

Her gaze skimmed the small army of servants cleaning up the kitchens, until it came to rest on Jonathan. The big knight stood talking to a man she could only guess was the head cook, who was eyeing him with a jaundiced eye and shaking his head firmly.

Jonathan, Lord Fairley, was not the sort to take no for an answer, though. As Alice watched, he talked and talked and smiled and charmed, then finally resorted to bribery. He pulled out a small sack of what Alice guessed were coins and pressed them on the man—whose attitude abruptly changed. The chef transformed from a narrow-eyed, grim-faced man to a jolly little cherub who pressed a basket on Jonathan and led him around stuffing food into it. Alice eased the door closed again.

When Lord Jonathan stumbled back out to rejoin her some moments later, he was bearing an overflowing basket and had a skin of wine tucked under his chin. Alice chuckled at the slightly stunned expression on his face, then relieved him of the wine.

"Accommodating fellow, was he not?" she asked with amusement. They moved up the hall.

"Aye, once I showed him some coin." He shook his head. "I think I may have been overgenerous."

Alice laughed softly. "Well, it did appear a hefty sack you offered him."

"I was so hungry, I would have given him half of Fairley Castle . . . and had begun to fear I might have to. He was not eager to indulge us." He chuckled.

Alice grinned at his tired jollity, then leaned toward him, poking at the contents of the basket as they walked. "What did he give you?"

"Everything." Lord Jonathan slowed a bit to adjust for her slightly staggered gait; she was trying to continue forward while twisting about to investigate the booty. "It would be easier to say what he did not give us."

Us. Alice left off poking through the basket, her gaze shooting quickly to the knight's face, then away as the word played in her mind. *Us. As if we were a couple,* she thought slowly as they exited the keep the same way they had entered. The idea pleased her immensely. In fact, the amount of pleasure it stirred in her was somewhat shocking. *Us.* She found herself smiling for no reason at all as she followed Jonathan through the darkness.

"Here. The perfect spot."

Pausing as he did, Alice glanced around the location he had chosen: a small clearing deep in the royal gardens. Two benches stood on either side of the path, one not far from a statue that seemed to gleam silver in the moonlight. It was that piece that finally told her where they were: this was the same clearing where she had first met Lord Jonathan, where he and his mother had joined her, her mother, and her uncle that first morning.

Her eyes slid slowly over the statue now. During daylight it appeared sweet, the woman bearing a sad, loving expression. Now, with moonlight casting shadows over it, it looked different. Rather than poignant, the statue's expression seemed seductive, that of a woman calling to a lover. The gown, which had seemed perfectly respectful and demure in daylight, seemed to cling and emphasize a lush shape.

"Ah."

Alice turned her attention from the statue to Jonathan. He had settled on the bench they had occupied that first day, and he was withdrawing items from the basket and setting them in the center of the bench. Giving up her position before the statue, Alice moved closer, smiling as he oohed and ahhed over their treasure. It appeared he hadn't paid much attention to whatever the chef had pressed into the basket, for he was obviously pleasantly surprised by many of the items he set out.

"Ahhhh, a feast worthy of a king." He sighed as he placed the last foodstuff on the bench and set the container aside.

"My, yes." Alice gazed over the fare with wide eyes. "Just how heavy was that purse you gave the chef?"

"Too heavy, apparently." The big knight chuckled. "Come sit."

He patted the empty portion of the bench, on the other side of the food from himself, then lifted a chicken leg and offered it to her as she sat. Alice accepted the offering, surprised to find she truly was quite hungry. They ate in companionable silence for several moments; then, as their hunger eased, they began to talk.

ALICE WAS EATING a fruit tart when it happened. The pastry crumbled slightly as she bit into it, smearing some of the berry filling on her cheek by the corner of her mouth. Chuckling, Jonathan leaned forward to catch up the sticky goo with a finger, then unthinkingly stuck that finger into his mouth. Apparently affected by the action, Alice stared at him, wide-eyed. Her expression made Jonathan aware of what he had just done, and their gazes met in one meaningful moment of silent communication.

"It is a pleasant night," Alice blurted then, setting the rest of her tart down on the bench.

"Aye." Jonathan gazed around, then up at the sky. "A clear, starry night, though there is a cool breeze. Are you chilled?"

Alice started to shake her head no, then realized that she was absently rubbing her upper arms. She shrugged. "A little. But not enough to wish to give up this lovely evening."

Jonathan frowned, not wishing her to suffer discomfort, but not wishing to bring an end to this interlude, either. He took a moment to marvel over the fact that she had admitted as much, herself. But then, he had noted that natural honesty in her quite early. Alice had a strong sense of truth and honor. She had staunchly refused to participate in spying on his mother and her uncle, Lord Houghton. After a hesitation, he removed his cape and settled it around her shoulders.

"Oh, but then you will be cold," she protested, trying to remove the gift.

"Nay, your very presence warms me," he said quietly. Replacing the garment around her shoulders and smiling at the softening of her expression, Jonathan hesitated, then used the cape to draw her closer.

This time there was no sudden arrival of his mother or hers, no interruption to stop him at all, and he let a small sigh slip from his lips as his mouth settled over hers. Her mouth was as soft and pliant as he expected, and he spent a moment just enjoying the warm feel of her before sliding his tongue out, questing for hers. Much to his pleasure, her lips opened at once. He suspected it was more from surprise than an understanding of what he was requesting, for while she allowed her mouth to slide open, she started to retreat at once in surprise.

Smiling against her mouth, Jonathan lifted his hand to the back of her neck, ending her retreat, then kissed her as he had imagined doing since the picnic. After one startled moment, Alice joined in. Her response was definitely lacking in skill, but was enthusiastic nonetheless. Jonathan spent several moments teaching her. By the time the lesson was over and he broke the kiss, they were both breathless and panting.

"Oh, my." Alice gasped shakily as they stared at each other in the moonlight.

"Aye," Jonathan murmured. He brushed a thumb gently over the side of her face; then, because he simply couldn't resist her passion-swollen lips, he bent to kiss her again. She was a quick learner; this time there was no need for tutelage, and she opened her mouth without his bidding, inviting him to deepen the kiss. Her boldness made the blood surge in Jonathan, but when she shifted instinctively closer, pressing her upper body into his, he gave up what little restraint he had and let his hands begin to explore. The hand at the back of her head slid down over the curve of her shoulder, sliding partway across her arm before drifting around to cross their bodies and cover one breast.

Alice promptly stiffened, her breath catching on a small gasp that briefly sucked the air out of his mouth; then her kisses became more frantic. Her arms wrapped around his neck and clutched almost desperately there as he squeezed and fondled until he could feel her nipple grow hard through her gown.

"Oh, please," she said softly against his cheek as he let his lips break away from hers. He slid them along the curve of her jaw. "Oh, ahhhh."

Jonathan smiled against her throat as her head dropped back, her breath coming in violent little pants as he sucked and nibbled at her tender flesh. Then she raised her head abruptly, desperately seeking his questing mouth for another kiss. Jonathan gave her what she wanted, his kisses less gentle and more devouring. His other hand slid down her waist and across her hip over the material of her gown then slowly shifted around to the inside of her leg. She didn't seem to notice what he was doing at first, her senses preoccupied with his other caresses, but when he reached the apex of her thighs and touched her there, she jumped, breaking the kiss with a start. Her eyes went round and uncertain.

Jonathan kept his hand still, allowing her to get used to its presence, and managed what he hoped was a gentle smile before he again brushed his lips lightly over hers. When she remained passive under that caress, neither protesting nor participating in his kiss, he brushed her lips again. He let his mouth drift over to her ear and set to work, nipping and tugging at the soft, plump lobe, then at the sensitive spot behind.

"Ohhhh." The word came out on a quavering sigh as Alice melted beneath his caresses. Jonathan felt relief rush through him. He was hard with desire from just their kisses, and he felt sure he would die if he had to stop now. She was an innocent, of course, and he knew he could not take this too far, but he felt sure that he could control himself. He would just go a little further, enjoy this beauty's awakening passion a little more. Touch her, and taste her, and ... Dear God, he wanted her as he had wanted no other woman before. But Jonathan knew he couldn't take her innocence. He renewed his assault on her throat and ear, then began to apply pressure between her legs, pressing the material of her gown against her. Rubbing slightly, he slid his tongue into her mouth once more.

ALICE WAS DYING of pleasure. Her eyes were open, staring blindly up at the stars above as Lord Jonathan did delicious things to her. She knew he should not do these things, but her body was clamoring under his gentle assault, and she seemed helpless to stop him. In fact, when the hand between her legs slid away, she nearly sobbed in protest. She caught her lower lip between her teeth to prevent such wanton behavior.

Her teeth bit down in surprise when Alice felt his hand actually touch the naked flesh of her calf. He had not stopped, but had dragged her skirt up and slid his hand under to glide gently over her knee to the sensitive skin of her thigh. A nervous giggle slid from her mouth into his, and she squirmed slightly from the tingles radiating out from his caress. His hand returned to its former position—between her legs. And this time, there was nothing to shield her from his touch.

Alice moaned long and low into his mouth, bucking slightly beneath this new caress as his fingers dipped into the slick core of her.

The sensations racing through her then were over- whelming. Alice was hardly aware when he used his other hand to drag her lower body across the remnants of their picnic. She was soon thigh-to-thigh with him. His mouth covered hers again, and he pressed her back as his touch became more aggressive.

They hardly noticed their tumble from the bench. Lord Jonathan took just enough notice to twist them so that he landed on the bottom with her splayed atop him; then he rolled her onto her back, his mouth dropping to cover her breast through her gown.

Alice felt the moist heat through the cloth, then heard Jonathan curse before he removed the hand between her legs to use both hands to tug at the top of her clothing. Missing that touch, Alice promptly began to help him, tugging and shimmying until her breasts were bared to his attentions. She groaned and arched when his mouth latched onto one swollen nipple, then twisted and arched again as his hand found its way back under her skirt and moved directly back to where she wanted it. The combi- nation left her completely mindless, a twisting, trembling mass beneath him.

"Please," she said in a gasp, reduced to begging. "Please, oh, Jonathan, please."

She thrust into his caress instinctively, her hands moving over what she could reach of him; his head, his hair, his shoulders and upper arms. She thrashed her legs restlessly until he cast one of his own over hers, nudging them apart and holding them still at the same time. Then she felt something begin to press deep into her, and she bucked in shock. Alice glanced down, thoroughly confused when she saw that Lord Jonathan still lay half on her and half off, fully clothed, only his hand between her legs. It took a moment for her to deduce that it was his finger inside her, and it was such an odd sensation that she went still, unsure whether she liked it or not. She did know that she missed his caress of a moment before, but then the caress started up again, similar but different, and she cried out in gratitude. Some part of her mind was guessing that he was using his thumb, but for the most part, her brain was beyond caring or thinking what he was doing so long as he didn't stop. She began to shift and thrust into his touch, clenching her hands into his hair to draw his mouth up for a kiss she desperately needed.

He accommodated her, and the kiss was as fiery and passionate as she'd yearned for. The next moment, Alice tore her mouth away to cry out as pleasure ripped through her. Her inner muscles contracted and vibrated, her thighs clenching around Lord Jonathan's hand, her arms and fingers tightening, her heart seeming to stop. When she regained herself enough to become aware of what was going on around her, it was to find Jonathan gently holding her, murmuring calming words as he pressed gentle kisses on her face.

"I—" Alice began, feeling shame and embarrassment slowly make their inevitable appearance, but her lover shushed her at once. He pressed a soothing kiss to her lips.

"Jonathan!"

Their kiss ended abruptly at that scandalized cry. A scramble ensued as Lord Jonathan quickly tugged her skirt down and sat up, shifting to block Alice from view. She tried desperately to straighten her gown.

"Mother!" There was no mistaking Lord Jonathan's outrage at this interruption, Alice decided as she struggled to right her clothing with hands that shook with humiliation.

"Do not 'Mother' *me* as though I am the one in the wrong, son. How *could* you?"

"I think you had best come with me, Alice."

Finished with her gown, Alice stiffened at those words. She sat up to peer reluctantly over Lord Jonathan's shoulder. A little sigh escaped her at the sight of her mother with Lady Fairley. It just figured the woman would be here to witness her daughter's shame, Alice thought unhappily. The only positive point at that moment, it seemed to Alice, was that Uncle James was not also in attendance.

"Alice."

Grimacing at her mother's tone of voice, Alice got reluctantly to her feet and moved around Lord Jonathan to follow Lady Houghton as she turned abruptly and started back up the path.

"Wait! Alice."

A glance over her shoulder showed Jonathan struggling to his feet to pursue her. Eager to be away from the scene of her humiliation, Alice did not stop, but she did slow down enough for him to catch up. Much to her relief, her mother continued on, unaware that her daughter was no longer on her heels. Alice had one brief moment in which she thought she might get a word alone with Jonathan to reassure herself that he did not think as poorly of her as everyone else apparently did, but it was only one moment; she glanced back to see Lady Fairley step into her son's path.

"Let her go!" the woman said, in a hiss. "I have told you all along that girl is not good enough for you, and now here I find her tossing about on the ground with you like some tavern wench out for a quick roll in the hay."

That was all Alice needed to hear. She had found Lady Fairley's treatment of her to be strange all along. The woman was pleasant enough when her son was not around, but cold when he was. Alice had wondered at that behavior, but now she understood. Lady Fairley disliked her. That dislike was obvious in the woman's tone just now. And her words had left little confusion over why.

Turning away, her eyes burning with tears, Alice ran through the darkness to catch up to her mother. The sweet interlude she had just experienced with Jonathan was suddenly a dirty, shameful thing, and the brief hopes for the future it had engendered in her died an abrupt death.

"Do NOT SAY another word or I swear, Mother, I shall—" Jonathan paused and swallowed the bile in his throat, trying to swallow his rage along with it. He had never felt anything close to the fury that had swamped him as his mother had insulted Alice. He had even actually started to raise his hand, preparing to slap her for saying what she had, but then had caught it back. Clenching it at his side, he told himself that Alice had left; the words could not hurt her so long as she had not heard them—and she would never hear them. Ever. Now he took a deep breath and glared at his mother coldly. "I am aware of your feelings regarding Alice. You have made them clear many times. However, I suggest you attempt to get over them, because first thing on the morrow, I intend to ask her to marry me."

On that note, he turned and strode briskly from the clearing.

Chapter Five

"ALICE!"

"Oh, damn," Alice muttered under her breath, recognizing that voice. She didn't need to look over her shoulder to know that Lord Jonathan was riding up behind her; she could hear the thunder of his horse's hooves. To be honest, she had rather hoped that taking herself away from the palace for the day would help her avoid him. One day: that was all she had hoped for, one day to compose herself and prepare to have to face him after last night's shameful conclusion.

It appeared it was too much to ask for.

He drew up alongside her and reached over to catch at the reins of her mount. "I have been looking for you all morning," he said accusingly as he drew her horse and his own to a halt. "*Everyone* has been looking for you. Even your mother had no idea where you had gone."

"I thought a ride would be nice. I . . ." Her words died abruptly when he suddenly leaned across the distance separating them and pressed his lips to hers. For a moment Alice went stiff, but then she softened with a moan and kissed him back.

"Good morn, my lady," he murmured huskily a moment later.

Alice opened her eyes. "Good morn," she answered solemnly.

"I would like to thank you."

His words made her blink. "For what, my lord?"

"For last night."

She immediately flushed with a combination of embarrassment and shame. He then urged his mount closer, attempting to hug her and pull her off of her mount onto his own at the same time, but she evaded him by urging her mare sideways. "Please, my lord. I—"

"Surely you can call me Jonathan," he chided gently, allowing her to escape him for the moment.

"I think it would be better if I did not."

"As you wish," he said mildly. "Howbeit, once the wedding is over, I will insist on your calling me Jonathan—at least in private."

Alice stilled, her uncertain gaze finding and locking on his. "The wedding? You have chosen a bride?"

"I have chosen you. If you will have me."

For one sweet moment, Alice's heart seemed to dance out of her chest with joy. Then, as thoughts of Lady Fairley intruded, it landed back in place with a bump that caused her actual pain.

"Alice?" Jonathan asked worriedly when she remained silent. "You *will* marry me, will you not?"

"Nay."

"Nay?" He stared at her blankly. "But . . . I realize we have not known each other long, but I thought that we got along rather well, and—"

"'Tis not you, Jonathan," she said gently. "I would marry you in a heartbeat, were it not for—"

"What?" he asked, catching her arms as if expecting her to flee.

"Your mother," she said quietly.

Lord Jonathan's hands dropped away weakly, his expression becoming one of defeat. "My mother."

"I am afraid so. She dislikes me greatly. I know that."

"Nay, she—"

"I heard what she said last night," Alice interrupted, bringing his protest to a halt. She watched rage flood over his features; then he paled and glanced away. A helpless look overcame his face. She guessed it meant that he realized he could not argue; she had already overheard the truth.

"'Tis not my mother you would be marrying," he said finally, an almost pleading look on his face as he turned back.

"Nay. I know. But did I marry you, I would have to live with her and her dislike of me forever." Pained by the look in his eyes, she reached out to caress his cheek gently as she tried to make him understand. "I love you, Jonathan, but I could not bear a life with a mother-in-law who hates me. My mother had that. My father's mother made her miserable. She made us all miserable with her constant and open hatred of my mother when I was young. It was like living on a battlefield where words were used in place of swords. I could not bear that. I am sorry."

"And I know you love your mother. I saw it in the way you were so protective of her when she was with Uncle James. I would do nothing to see that relationship destroyed." Retrieving her reins from his slack hands, she turned her mare and started back toward court at a canter. She didn't look back at the possible future she was leaving behind, and Jonathan let her go.

"MOTHER!"

"Oh, dear." Lady Fairley rushed across the room, plopped onto the stool by the fire, and snatched up her hairbrush just as Jonathan crashed into the chamber.

"Good morn, son," she said waspishly, pulling the brush through her hair with studied indifference. "I suppose you have proposed to that girl?"

"Aye."

Margaret barely restrained herself from leaping from her seat with a victorious shout, and had to take a moment to calm herself before she could speak. "And when is the wedding to be?" She asked at last, affecting a sneer. Five years of planning, and at last her scheme had met with success!

"Never. She refused me."

Lady Fairley leaped to her feet after all, but her roar was far from victorious. "*What?*"

"I said, she refused me," he repeated.

"Well, why?" Lady Fairley gasped. "Surely she does not think herself too good for you, does she?"

"Nay. She thinks she is too good for you," he snapped.

That took her aback, and Margaret sank onto her stool in dismay. "What?"

"Alice knows you do not like her. She overheard your slurs and insults about her last night."

"Oh . . . I see." Lady Fairley bit her lip under her son's accusatory glare, then rallied. "Well, that hardly matters. 'Tis not me she will be marrying."

"Which is exactly what I argued. However, it seems that Lady Houghton, her mother, apparently suffered under a hateful mother-in-law who did not like her. Alice's grandmother made Alice, her mother, and father miserable with her hatred of Lady Houghton. Alice has no wish to repeat history . . . so refuses to marry me. Because of you."

"Oh, dear. I had forgotten about that," Margaret muttered under her breath. She frowned.

"What?" Jonathan glanced at her sharply, and Margaret turned her glower on him.

"Never mind. I shall take care of this," she announced, setting down her brush.

"What? How?" he asked sharply, following her to the door.

"I shall have James find her and send her here to talk to me."

Her big knight of a son threw his hands up helplessly. "Oh, *that* will be of great assistance. I may as well go tell the king to pick me a bride. You shall scare her off completely if you interfere."

"Nonsense." Margaret smiled, sure she could help. "Have a little faith in your mother."

ALICE LECTURED HERSELF grimly all the way to Lady Fairley's chamber. She really had no desire to see the woman who had ruined her happiness, let alone speak to her. However, her uncle had found her in the small alcove where she'd been indulging in self-pity and tears, alternately berating herself for giving up the happiness she might have enjoyed with Jonathan, and assuring herself that she had made the right choice. A mother-in-law who hated her would have made both their lives miserable.

Always having been uncomfortable with tears, her uncle had shifted anxiously about, his gaze landing everywhere but on her as he had announced that she was to go directly to Lady Fairley's chamber. He had made it clear that this was an order from her mother that was not to be brooked and that dallying was out of the question.

For one moment, Alice had considered rebelling against her uncle's command to visit Lady Margaret, but then had decided she did not have the energy. Now she found herself pausing outside the door of the nasty witch who had ruined her life. She had no idea why she had been summoned here, but had no doubt it had something to do with Jonathan. Alice supposed it was possible that he had informed his mother of his intention to propose, and that this was some attempt by Lady Fairley to be sure Alice said no when he did. Of course, there was no need for such a request now, but perhaps Jonathan had not yet informed his mother of Alice's refusal. Which left it up to her to do. *Great.*

Taking a deep breath, she pasted a nonchalant smile on her face and tapped on the door.

"Enter."

Alice grimaced at the command, but quickly replaced her anger with a more pleasant, though less honest, smile. She opened the door.

"Ah, Alice." Lady Fairley stood up from her seat by the fire and started across the room. Oddly enough, she wore a welcoming smile on her face. Which served only to make Alice warier. "Thank you for coming, I—"

"You need not fear, my lady. I am not going to marry Jonathan," Alice blurted. The older woman's smile faded and she halted as if struck by a lance.

Quite sure the woman would be grateful to hear the news, Alice was wholly unprepared when Lady Fairley roared, "Oh, yes, you are!"

Alice blinked in surprise, sure she had misunderstood. "I beg your pardon?"

"My dear girl, I have worked too long and too hard to get the two of you together to have you refuse Jonathan now."

Alice gaped. "Excuse me?"

"You heard me. Sit down."

Confusion reining in her poor, woolly mind, Alice sat on the nearest item of furniture, the end of Lady Fairley's bed. She watched in bewilderment as Lady Fairley began to pace.

"First off," Jonathan's mother said abruptly, "I wish to know if you love my son. Or think you can grow to love him."

"I . . . yes," she stammered, too bewildered to lie. "I do."

"Good." But the satisfied smile that came to Lady Fairley's face did not reassure Alice. "I can explain. Jonathan is a wonderful boy: intelligent, charming, handsome, loving . . . every mother's delight. But he does have one flaw. He is as stubborn and contrary as his father ever was."

"That would be two flaws, my lady. And I have already noticed them," Alice agreed. Lady Fairley knelt down by her side at once.

"Of course you did, you brilliant girl!" She took Alice's hands in her own as she rose and settled on the edge of the bed next to her. "And even with these flaws you will love him."

"No one is perfect, my lady. And as flaws go, stubbornness and a contrary nature are rather typical of men."

"Aye." Lady Fairley sighed. "However, I doubt you have quite grasped the depth of his stubborn and contrary nature, especially when it comes to myself. I fear Jonathan is . . . constantly suspecting me of some scheme or another. And . . . well, were I to point out that the sky was blue, he would swear it was orange simply to avoid agreeing with me. Especially if he thought he might find himself ensnared in some imaginary plot."

"Oh, dear." Alice patted Lady Fairley's hand sympathetically. "That must be trying."

"Oh, my dear, you have no idea." Lady Fairley shook her head tragically, then heaved a sigh and went on. "So, seeing as how he was dallying about finding a bride, I— Oh!" She interrupted herself, giving a nervous laugh. "I mean, when the king gave the order for Jonathan to choose a bride within two weeks, well, I decided it was time I took a hand in his future. Two weeks is a very short time to find a bride. I knew he would take no advice from me, so . . ." She shrugged helplessly.

"So you schemed and plotted to aid him in the endeavor," Alice suggested.

"Aye." Lady Fairley beamed at her, apparently missing the irony in Alice's voice. "Your cleverness is one of the reasons I felt sure you would be perfect for him. And I did know you would be perfect, my dear. Oh, I introduced him to the daughters of various other friends, but I knew they would not catch his interest. I was simply giving him something to measure you by, knowing you would come out shining above the rest. Of course, I could not introduce you the same way. He would have rejected you whether he was interested or not, simply to confound me. I had to find a way to make him wish to be around you . . . So, your mother, and I—"

"Uncle James," Alice said softly as the realization struck.

Jonathan's mother nodded. "I fear I was not much taken with your uncle; however, he really did come through for us. And, to be honest, he was really only necessary the first day or two. After that, I do not think

Jonathan cared so much what I did. My plan was working beautifully; his attention was wholly taken up with you."

Alice digested that slowly. "Am I to understand that the courtship that you and my uncle were indulging in was all a sham meant somehow to convince Jonathan to ask me to marry him?"

"Aye."

Alice briefly chewed that claim over, then asked bluntly, "Why? You detest me."

"Detest you? Nay, child! I adore you. You will be a wonderful daughter-in-law. Why, you are clever and sweet and honest to the bone, and . . ." Pausing, Lady Fairley framed Alice's face with her hands and allowed a true affection to show through. "Alice, had I had a daughter of my own, instead of a son, I would have liked her to be you."

Alice felt tears well up inside her at that kind claim, but shook her head with confusion. "But I heard you telling Jonathan—"

"I am sorry, my dear." Lady Fairley interrupted with sincere regret. "Jonathan told me that you overheard me last night, but I never intended for you to be privy to that nonsense. What I said then was not at all true; I was simply misleading Jonathan. I was hoping to raise his interest by making him think I did not care for you."

"I see," Alice murmured, gazing down at her hands.

A moment of silence passed as Alice considered all she had learned; then Lady Fairley could stand it no longer. "So? You will marry my son?"

Alice lifted her head slowly and peered at Margaret for a long time; then she nodded. "Aye."

"Oh, lovely!" Jonathan's mother exclaimed, hugging her happily. "You are perfect for each other. I know you will be happy together. I—"

"On one condition."

Lady Fairley stiffened. "Condition?"

"Aye. As much as I appreciate that you love Jonathan, and that you want only the best for him . . . And as much as I appreciate how you got us together, I really must insist that the interference stop here, this very moment. I will not marry Jonathan if it means spending the rest of my life worrying about what you are up to."

"Oh, my dear." Smiling, Lady Margaret patted the girl's hands affectionately. "I will be more than happy to stop my interfering. All I wanted in the world was to see my boy happy, and I knew he could be very, very happy with you. Now that the two of you are together, there is no longer any necessity for me to interfere. I can happily retire and enjoy my golden years."

Alice relaxed and smiled. Her eyes growing misty, she squeezed the older woman's hands. "Thank you, then. For everything you have done."

"You are more than welcome, my dear." Lady Margaret hugged Alice briefly, then sat back and smiled. "Now, Jonathan is waiting in the garden where we found you last night. Go drag my son out of the misery your refusal has sunk him in. I promise, this time I shall not interrupt."

Beaming, Alice rose quickly and rushed from the room.

Lady Fairley watched the girl go, then opened the chest beside her with a pleased sigh.

"What are you doing now, Margaret?" Elizabeth of Houghton slid out from behind the curtains that had been hiding her for the past several minutes. Her best friend since childhood was drawing a piece of parchment and a quill and ink out of the chest.

"Setting to work on a plan to get Alice with child. All we need are grandbabies to make things perfect."

"From what I saw when we *finally* interrupted those two last night, babies will not be a problem," Elizabeth said dryly. She moved forward to look over her friend's shoulder at the list being written.

"I told you, it would not have done to stop them too early. Had Jonathan not already intended to wed Alice at that point, we would have been able to use what we saw to force them to marry. Which would not have been possible had we interrupted earlier," Lady Fairley said, sounding a touch irritated. "Besides, while they may be enthusiastic about the endeavor, one can never tell how the matter of fertility rests with the two of them. A little help in that area will not hurt." Then she glanced up with a twinkle in her eye. "I spent the better part of the winter investigating which herbs increase a woman's fertility, and which a man's ardor. . . . Just in case."

"When you were not plotting how to get the two together, and corresponding with me on the details of that plan?" Elizabeth asked dryly.

"'Twas a long winter, was it not?" came Lady Fairley's response. "And 'tis always nice to have a project to occupy the mind during such long, bitter winters."

"Hmm." Lady Houghton shook her head at her friend's antics, watching her draw up a list of ways to encourage grandchildren. "Did I not hear you vow mere moments ago never again to interfere in the lives of our children?"

"Oh, well. And I shan't . . . except for ensuring that I get grandbabies."

"But you swore on your honor." Lady Houghton taunted.

Margaret gave her a dry look. "Elizabeth, darling, you know that a mother lets nothing, not even her own needs, not even her honor, stand in the way of her child's happiness . . . and getting her grandbabies."

"ALICE!" JONATHAN LEAPED to his feet the moment he saw her approaching and silently blessed his mother for whatever it was she had said. Things must be fixed, for that was the only reason he could see that Alice would be there. He knew he was right when, as soon as she spied him, a smile bloomed on her face. She picked up her pace to run into his open arms.

"Oh, thank God," he said softly, holding Alice close and swinging her around in a half circle before setting her down. Peering down into her face in question, he asked, "Mother straightened everything out? You will marry me?"

"Aye." Alice laughed happily. "She explained everything, and really, she is a dear, Jonathan. You are very fortunate."

He goggled at the claim. "A dear? Fortunate? She nearly lost you for me."

"Nay. She loves you very much, Jonathan. And were it not for her help, we would not be together."

"Her help? Ha!" He scoffed at the very idea. "She did everything in her power to turn my attentions away from you. Had I listened to her, we never would have even met. Why, that first morning, she did everything in her power to dissuade me from accompanying her to the gardens where she was to meet you, your mother, and uncle."

"Which only made you more determined to accompany her," Alice pointed out gently.

Jonathan stopped his pacing to turn slowly toward Alice. The truth dawned on him. "She manipulated me."

Alice nodded apologetically. "She knew that if she asked you to accompany her to meet the daughter of a friend, you would balk. And that if she acted at all as if she thought I was suitable, you would find some excuse not to be interested in me. So she—"

"Played me false. She acted as though you were thoroughly unsuitable in her opinion and . . ." He narrowed his eyes. "Your uncle?"

"A trick, I fear," she admitted with more apology. "His attentions were false, something they stirred up between the three of them. It was intended to keep you around us long enough for you to get to know me."

"Your mother was in on this, too?" he asked in horror.

"Well . . ." Alice grimaced. "Your mother said that she was not, but I suspect she was: Mama is the only one who could have convinced Uncle James to participate."

"Damn." Jonathan sank slowly to sit on the bench. Alice peered at him, obviously worried.

"Jonathan? Are you all right? Has this changed things? Do you not wish to marry me after all?"

"What?" He glanced at her distractedly; then what she had said sank in. He leaped to his feet again. "Nay! I mean, aye! Aye, of course I still want to marry you. I just . . . well, I—" He made a face. "It is discomfiting to know I am so easily played by the woman."

Alice seemed amused by that comment when he suddenly whirled on her. "Did she admit to involvement in getting the king to order me to marry?"

"Er . . . well, no. That did not come up." She frowned briefly, then moved to stand in front of him. "But does it really matter, my lord? I mean, you do really want to marry me, do you not? 'Tis not simply a case of having to marry, and I am the most likely candidate . . . is it?"

Recognizing her fear, Jonathan took her hand. The last thing he wanted was for her to believe such nonsense. "Nay, Alice. You are not simply the most likely candidate. Even were there not a pressing need to marry, I would surely want to wed you. And most likely just as swiftly. In case you had not noticed, my passions become carried away whenever you are about."

She ducked her head and rubbed her fingers over the knuckles of his hand. "Actually, I had not noticed, my lord. It appeared to me last night that you were the one in control, and that I was the one carried away."

"That is only because my mother interrupted us," he assured her. "I kept telling myself that I could not take your innocence, that your satisfaction must be enough until I could get you properly wed to me. . . ." He grimaced.

"'Struth, I was a heartbeat away from ravishing you there on the ground like some lowborn wench."

Alice blushed, but smiled. "And are you sure you will not mind being married to such a wanton as myself?" At his uncertain look, she quietly admitted, "I fear I do not think I would have minded being ravished there on the ground. In fact, I would not protest should you wish to do so now."

Jonathan felt his body harden and tighten at the very suggestion. He swallowed thickly. Damn, just the thought of it had him ready for action. Hesitating briefly, he glanced around, gauging the odds of getting caught. They might be getting married, but they weren't yet. He wouldn't see her shamed before he—His thoughts died abruptly as he became aware of Alice's hand drifting down toward the more than obvious bulge between his legs.

"Perhaps," she murmured, meeting his startled gaze boldly, "you might even teach me to please you as you pleasured me, my lord. Your mother promised not to interrupt us this time."

"Oh, Alice, my sweet." Jonathan laughed. "Whether my mother was involved or not, you are definitely the right bride for me."

She smiled widely at those words and took his hand to lead him around the bench and toward the bushes behind it. "I am glad you think so, my lord. I, too, think we shall be terribly happy together."

"Until my mother next interferes," he added dryly.

"Oh, nay." Alice paused and leaned into his chest, her expression serious as she slid her hands up around his neck. She drew his head down for a kiss.

Jonathan's legs nearly gave out at the shock of her aggression. His lovely lady was a very quick learner! He let his arms slide around her and pressed his hands against her bottom, urging her up against his hardness. Her tongue delved into his mouth and explored with an abandon that left him trembling. He actually moaned aloud when she broke the kiss and leaned back to murmur, "She has vowed never to interfere again."

"Oh, that is all right then," he whispered huskily, then claimed her lips once more.

Jonathan had little real hope that his mother could fulfill that vow. The woman simply did not know how *not* to interfere. Still, he would keep that little tidbit to himself. He had no intention of scaring off the woman he loved. He was rather hoping that by the time Alice realized his mother simply did not have the nature to keep that promise, Alice would love her enough to overlook it. Lady Margaret of Fairley was a woman who grew on a person, and her intentions were always the best. She loved her son and wanted what was best for him. And this was one of the few times Jonathan agreed with his mother. As his new bride-to-be led him farther into the surrounding trees and bushes, he conceded Alice *was* definitely the best. And despite her interference, or perhaps because of it, so was his mother.

About the Author

LYNSAY SANDS is the nationally bestselling author of the Argeneau/Rogue Hunter vampire series, as well as numerous historicals and anthologies. She's been writing stories since grade school and considers herself incredibly lucky to be able to make a career out of it. Her hope is that readers can get away from their everyday stress through her stories, and if there are occasional uncontrollable fits of laughter, that's just a big bonus. Visit her official website at www.lynsaysands.net.

Visit www.AuthorTracker.com for exclusive information on your favorite HarperCollins authors.